Panic Swamped Her.

She retraced her steps and faced him, her heart pounding.

His eyes were closed. He looked so totally relaxed that she hated to disturb him. Gena pressed a hand to her heart, then raised it, lightly touching his forehead and temples, applying a soothing motion first with one hand, then with both. When her aching arms faltered after a minute, she was unable to stop them from sinking to his bare chest, her trembling fingers spreading out on his muscled, tan flesh.

"Don't stop." His eyes lifted to reveal a slumbrous longing. The hooded, steady gaze seemed to drink in the shadows near her unsure, startled eyes, her flushed cheeks, and the shocked parting of her mouth, moist where the tip of her tongue had touched it.

"I . . . I . . ." What had she been going to say? It didn't matter. Nothing mattered as he took her in his arms.

LORRAINE VALLEY

found it only natural to turn to writing romances because she has known so much love in her own life. This happily married mother of four loves to travel, and this is evident in the vividly presented places, inhabited by exciting men and women, that she chooses for her novels.

Dear Reader;

SILHOUETTE DESIRE is an exciting new line of contemporary romances from Silhouette Books. During the past year, many Silhouette readers have written in telling us what other types of stories they'd like to read from Silhouette, and we've kept these comments and suggestions in mind in developing SILHOUETTE DESIRE.

DESIREs feature all of the elements you like to see in a romance, plus a more sensual, provocative story. So if you want to experience all the excitement, passion and joy of falling in love, then SILHOUETTE DESIRE is for you.

I hope you enjoy this book and all the wonderful stories to come from SILHOUETTE DESIRE. I'd appreciate any thoughts you'd like to share with us on new SILHOUETTE DESIRE, and I invite you to write to us at the address below:

Jane Nicholls
Silhouette Books
PO Box 177
Dunton Green
Sevenoaks
Kent
TN13 2YE

LORRAINE VALLEY
Blanket of Stars

Silhouette Desire

Published by Silhouette Books

Copyright © 1982 by Lorraine Valley

First printing 1983

British Library C.I.P.

Valley, Lorraine
   Blanket of stars.—(Silhouette desire)
   I. Title
   813'.54[F]   PS3572.A/

   ISBN 0 340 32925 4

Printed and bound in Great Britain for
Hodder and Stoughton Paperbacks, a
division of Hodder and Stoughton Ltd.,
Mill Road, Dunton Green, Sevenoaks,
Kent (Editorial Office: 47 Bedford
Square, London, WC1 3DP) by
Richard Clay (The Chaucer Press) Ltd.,
Bungay, Suffolk

To Jack and my children

1

~oooooooooooo~

The Mediterranean-bound 747 took off from the rain-darkened tarmac into Kennedy Airport's overcast skies, heading out over the Atlantic.

There was no turning back now. Gena Fielding gave a quiet, resigned sigh and released her seat belt. Glancing quickly at her fellow passengers, she ruffled her silk suit jacket to shake out any would-be wrinkles, and then settled her slender shape back against the plush comfort of the padded chair. The forward section was only three-quarters full; she wasn't the only one without a seatmate. Not that she wanted a companion for the long flight; she had enough on her mind without having to listen to a stranger's chatter.

The jetliner was leaving the East Coast thunderclouds behind. Sunbeams danced off the gold of her wristwatch, a recent birthday gift from her father. Gena leaned closer to the window on her left. It looked as if they were flying over a cushion of cotton candy. Her thoughts turned wistful as she continued to admire the white, fleecy shapes. If only . . .

The cheery voice of a stewardess interrupted her private musings. Would she like coffee, a magazine? Gena forced a smile in return, shedding for a moment the troubled expression that had shone in her wide, violet eyes since today's early morning phone call.

"Just coffee, please," she answered, self-consciously lifting a hand to smooth back a long wisp of dark brown hair that had come loose from its sophisticated swirl. After the steaming cup had been placed on a tray in front of her, she let it cool for a while before sipping its contents, meanwhile allowing her attention to drift back toward the window.

By rights, her trip to Greece should have been a joyous one, a reunion with the grandmother that she hadn't seen in many years. When her mother was alive they had flown to the Aegean Islands every Easter, without fail, but it was understandable that her father hadn't allowed the visits to continue. After all, a man couldn't very well ship his only child across the sea and into the clutches of his eldest brother-in-law, who was also his employer, the man who had wrongly blamed him for Gena's mother's accidental death, telling him so to his face after the funeral and then having him followed by a private investigator for months to come.

Gena knew that she was not a nervous type, but hearing Alex Andreas' cold, brusque tones over the phone at six o'clock this morning, bluntly informing her that her grandmother was seriously ill and wished to see her, had made her legs quiver alarmingly. Her father had intervened at that point, furnishing their long-distance caller with Gena's travel plans when it became evident that he had no knowledge of the letter she had recently sent to Madame Andreas, accepting the long-standing invitation she had extended to Gena in her letters, an invitation she now felt almost cruel in answering.

At least there was one good thing—the wealthy shipping tycoon's home office was in Kifissia, a northern suburb of Athens, and not on his mother's island paradise in the Cyclades, some one hundred miles southeast, where Ana, his six-year-old daughter, spent most of the year. Gena smiled; she could hardly wait to make friends with the little girl. They shared a bond of sorts—Ana's mother had also died.

As she reached for her cup, her hand trembled. *Who was she trying to kid?* Why pretend that she belonged inside that exclusive family circle? She wasn't Greek—she wasn't even her mother's daughter. The brown liquid sloshed toward the edge of the cup as she replaced the mug on its tray and thought back to that scene with her father, a scene that would forever be engraved on her mind.

* * *

9

"Your mother never knew," James Fielding had chokingly hastened to explain, his usually ruddy complexion turning a pasty gray. He had come upon her while she was probing the depths of his safe for her passport. "Ava was so weak from the delivery of our own daughter that the doctor considered it unwise to tell her . . . that the baby had not survived." His voice had broken as he gathered her close, kneeling beside her sobbing body. "You were a godsend, Gena. Via the hospital grapevine, our doctor learned that a young, unmarried woman had put her baby up for immediate adoption. Ava always believed that you were hers. She never knew . . . never once suspected," he had repeated, trying to console her. "I've wanted to tell you, but just couldn't. I was sure you'd hate me. Maybe someday you'll understand and forgive me." He helped her to her feet. "I loved her so much. . . ."

Gena had accepted the tissue he handed her, one hand still clutching the yellowed packet of documents bearing the seal of the state of New York.

"You were . . . a school teacher when . . . you met."

He had nodded. "And she was eighteen and beautiful. She had come to New York with her father, intending to shop and sightsee while Takis attended a week of meetings. I wandered into Sotheby's auction house on Madison Avenue and there she was. Her bodyguard positively bristled when I sat next to her."

"Yet you returned to Greece with them," she had pointed out.

"We were married there—within a month."

This had been news to Gena. She suddenly forgot her own misery.

"Ava told her parents that we had been intimate. It was untrue, but it had the desired effect. The wedding was arranged as quickly as possible. Alex, only fifteen at the time, must have overheard the gossip. His grudge against me goes back a long way. I think he even blames me for causing the stroke that killed his father. It happened shortly after I called to tell the family about Ava's accident."

It was dark when they landed at Hellenikon Airport near Athens' urban sprawl. While she waited her turn to pass through Customs, she glanced about the impressive, white marble complex with a searching look. There was no sign of anyone officially representing the Andreas family, nor had her name been broadcast over the call system, directing her to such a person.

Gena had no difficulty in finding a taxi to take her the few miles into the heart of the city. The Greek capital had an abundance of transportation for hire, it seemed, though several times along some of the busy avenues she found herself praying that the slightly wheezy rattletrap she had settled on would get her to the Hilton in one piece.

At first she hadn't wanted her father to book a room for a full week at the gracefully situated hotel, especially after she found out that she was to be met at Hellenikon. One night would have been sufficient, she had thought. But now, with no friendly face in sight, she was grateful that he had had the foresight to do so. Who knew how long she might be left here on her own?

After tipping the porter for helping her with her luggage, Gena secured the door and flung off her beige silk jacket, draping it over a blue damask chair, and then asked the Hilton's switchboard for assistance to call New York.

When the connection was made and Gena explained her circumstances, James immediately voiced his surprised concern, ordering her to get in touch with Andreas Shipping first thing in the morning.

She was tense by the time she put the phone down so, to relax her tired muscles, she took a luxurious soak in the beautiful black Carrara marble tub. It was past midnight when she slipped under the covers, after taking one last look down the Athenian hillside at the Royal Palace and the Parthenon, directly in view from her balcony.

She awakened early. The morning air was already warm. And even though it was six in the morning, she knew that many of Athens' three million inhabitants were already beginning their day.

What would the next twenty-four hours bring for her, she wondered, not without some apprehension, as she stood looking over the city. Hopefully, she would make some contact with her mother's family. Instant tears started. If only they were *her* family. She must have cursed herself a thousand times during the past days for opening Pandora's box, so to speak.

What's done is done. Nothing can undo the past, so the only thing to do is make the best of it, was her practical thought. For a while she stood and watched the sun making its shimmering ascent in the sky, flooding the city with a reddish tinge.

Then she shut the doors and padded across the thick carpet toward the bathroom. After taking a quick, refreshing shower, she lightly applied powder to her tanned features, followed by a glossy lipstick and a touch of pale smudged shadow to her eyelids. Her makeup finished, she reached for an elastic-waisted flared skirt that matched her scoopnecked lavender top. Both were made of a smooth cottony material that resisted wrinkles—just the fabric to wear in a warm climate.

She brushed her hair back, clasping it at her nape with a wide wooden hair clip. Satisfied with her cool-looking appearance, she slipped neutral-toned leather sandals on. There was still plenty of time to have a leisurely breakfast before making her call. Or perhaps she could inquire about finding her own way to the island.

Just then a sharp rap on her door startled her.

"Who is it?" she asked cautiously.

"Gena?" A baritone voice called. "I have come to bring you to the island."

Gena had mixed feelings as she unlocked the

door. A pleased grin lit the face of the curly-haired Greek who entered the small sitting room. His brown eyes obviously appreciated what they saw.

He flashed her a brilliant, white smile. "What a lovely niece I have!" He took hold of her bare arms, holding her firmly so that she had no choice but to look directly into his face. He was exactly her height as she stood in two-inch heels. This couldn't be . . .

"I have not seen you since you were a very little girl."

Gena cleared her throat, partly in relief. "You must be Uncle Nick, then."

He laughed. "You thought I was Alex? Heaven forbid!" He dropped his hands, motioning to the chairs that graced the well-appointed room. "Let us sit. We have much to tell one another."

When they were seated, he said, with hesitation in his tone, "I was supposed to have been at the airport last night. Can you forgive me for not doing my duty? If Alex ever found out, he would have my head, I know it." He grimaced.

Gena nodded, but deep down she was just a little hurt that this charming man could have forgotten about her.

"It's all right," she replied stiffly.

Her true feelings must have shown in her violet eyes, because he said unhappily, "Please forgive me. I didn't forget you, but Alex couldn't come and I had things I had to do."

"Don't concern yourself about making excuses

for *him*. I know how Uncle Alex feels about my father and me."

"You do?" He regarded her in surprise. "Then tell me why he feels as he does. I am still puzzled. I have never understood why he seems so bitter."

"I . . . I think there were bad feelings long ago," she explained lamely.

"When your papa and my sister were wed? Ahhh, yes. I see. . . ." He pondered this for a moment, then said abruptly, "Do you want to hear the truth about why I wasn't waiting for you at the airport last evening? I was with a girl. . . . But don't tell Alex."

Gena hid a smile. It seemed even Nick was wary of his brother's temper.

"Yes, you see," he continued, "I have a girlfriend who lives in the city. After eating out last night, we . . . Well, you understand."

"Please. Don't say another word." Gena could feel her face turning a bright shade of pink. "You don't have to share your private life with me, Uncle Nick!"

"But must you call me that? I'm not even thirty yet, and that 'uncle' makes me feel as old as Methuselah! I don't mind little Ana calling me that, of course, but . . ."

"I understand . . . really," she nodded, trying hard not to laugh outright. What would he say if she told him that she wasn't really his niece? The thought sobered her instantly.

"Good. Shall we go to breakfast now? After we

eat, I shall fly us to the villa." He got to his feet politely as Gena rose. "Thank heavens I found you so quickly. This was only the second hotel I called. When I awoke at six this morning I panicked, wondering where you were. It amazes me that I am properly attired," he said, shaking his dark head of hair. Then, in a bantering tone, he pleaded, "If anyone—namely my brother—ever asks, lie a little, won't you? Tell him that I was at the airport, that I safely escorted you to your hotel room, and then returned for you in the morning hours, as planned."

Gena nodded absentmindedly. "Does Grandmother know I'm coming today?" she asked in a subdued tone.

"I am almost sure that she does." His reply was equally sober, and lines of strain suddenly appeared around his mouth.

"How long has she been ill? What's wrong?"

"It has only been a month or so that she has been noticeably sick," he explained gravely. "It is her heart. The doctors think that she has had a heart problem for many years, but that she has kept it to herself so that we would not worry."

"But why isn't she in a hospital?" Gena cried. "She could be having treatment. Surely something can be done."

"Mother needs an operation, but she refuses to leave the island. She has told us that she would rather die in her own bed." Nick jammed his tanned hands deep into his pockets, his downcast eyes rimmed with pain. "Come on," he urged tightly. "Let's go. We can return later for your luggage. To save time we will eat here."

An hour and a half later their helicopter began its journey to the island. It was a breathtaking way to start a day, Gena found. Her legs weakened as she peered down at the hot, white-washed ancient city, now far below their four-passenger craft. When at last they were over the deep blue of the Aegean, Nick startled her with his half-shout, as he raised his voice to speak to her over the steady drone of the aircraft's motor.

"Do you remember anything of your previous visits here?"

Gena's lips curved. "Oh, yes!" she replied enthusiastically. "I loved them. It was always so beautiful on the island. The flowers, especially the smell of myrtle, and the sun and swimming. I never wanted to return to New York, but Mother would always say, 'We'll come again next year.'"

"Poor little Gena. It must have been difficult for you when my sister died. Mother has worried about you over the succeeding years, you know. It was most distressing to her when your father refused to bring you here every year as Ava did. There has been a severe lack of communication between our two families. . . ."

"Grandmother and I have been corresponding," Gena put in quickly.

"I know. Alex and I usually read your letters to her."

17

Her mouth formed a small, shocked 'O.' There were times she had written about some rather personal topics! Color mounted in her cheeks.

"Don't be upset. You write lovely letters," he assured her. He went on to explain, "You see, Mother can't read English as well as she'd like, though she speaks it reasonably well, so Alex and I do our part by helping her if we're around. She refuses to have a secretary underfoot, which is why weeks sometimes pass before she answers you."

"When I planned this trip I had no idea that Grandmother was ill. Uncle Alex phoned my father just before we left for the airport. That's when I found out she was sick."

Nick reached over and patted her hand. "And if I know my brother, he was not subtle. I imagine you were shocked. We aren't on the best of terms, he and I. He thinks I'm wasting my life, that I am not serious enough. That I am—how do you say?—frittering my life away."

Gena nodded her understanding, her eyelids drooping. She saw Nick give her a quick, knowledgeable look.

"Don't hesitate to nap if you're sleepy. You've had an exciting few days; a short rest will do you good." He flashed her a smile. "And don't worry. When I sight the island, I'll give you a nudge!"

She gratefully closed her eyes, resting her head against the soft leather headrest, and was soon asleep. Later, Nick woke her with a light tap on the shoulder and pointed straight ahead. "There it is—the island."

She strained her eyes to see, excitement filling
her. "Yes. Yes, I see it. . . . Oh, the trees. They look
so big now. They were such little things when I was
last here. I helped plant a couple of them, you
know." She shivered, almost overcome with happiness. "Do you think Grandmother will really be
happy to see me?"

"I promise you she will be delighted."

They passed through a cloud, moving closer to
the sapphire-shaded water as they did so.

"The villa looks bigger," she commented.

"Yes. We've added a few more rooms for Ana."

Gena looked at him curiously. "Does she have a
nanny?"

"No. One of our housekeeper's daughters looks
after her when she needs supervision."

They flew the length of the island, much to
Gena's great satisfaction, before returning to drop
onto the helicopter landing pad, a good, brisk walk
from the house.

"Did I see someone walking on the beach back
there? Who was it?" she asked as the great over-
head blades whirred to a stop.

"Alex."

"Oh," she commented, her heart beating a trifle
faster. "I thought he lived in Athens."

Nick opened his door after unstrapping his seat-
belt. "Not since Mother's illness."

Soon they were both following the large, flat
stone path leading to the sprawling villa. The sun
felt hot and relentless as it beat down on her bare
neck.

Nick paused, waiting for her to catch up to him. He had insisted on carrying both suitcases, despite her protests.

"Be careful how you walk. Some of these stones need replacing." Then, "It certainly is a good thing that you have already acquired a light tan. I should hate to see you burn." He laughed. "Little Ana is as brown as a nut."

"I can hardly wait to see her."

Concerned, he saw her touch her damp forehead. "Come." He set down one of the cases as they reached an outside door. "It will be much cooler in the house."

And it was. Blessedly cooler. And quiet. Gena's next words dropped to a whisper. "Where is everyone? Are they all resting before lunch?"

"It is very possible," he admitted, though he looked a little worried. "I hope Mother . . ." He stopped speaking abruptly. "But of course if something was wrong, we would have been greeted and told," he continued practically. "The nurse would have left word."

"I didn't know you had hired a nurse."

"It was necessary. Mother needs medication. She is also on a strict diet and needs bed baths and so on. Alex brought Miss Vouzas from Athens." He smiled at Gena. "You will meet her later, I am sure. She is a very nice young woman. Now, follow me. I think I know which room is to be yours."

"The villa is even lovelier than I remembered," she murmured, half to herself, as she followed Nick, gazing admiringly around the airy, spacious living area. "And what a gorgeous carpet!" She stopped at once to look more closely at the room's large rug, its intricate, beautiful pattern obviously hand-woven.

Over his shoulder, Nick volunteered, "The proper name for that particular kind of rug is flokati. It's virgin wool, woven in Western Thessaly where carftsmen have produced beauties like that since the age of Odysseus. I believe Alex bought it several years ago. It improves with age, unlike him." He grinned devilishly as he led the way into a lengthy hall, dotted with a myriad of doors.

Gena pretended not to hear his last words. But her heart beat a little faster. For a few minutes she had almost forgotten about Alex's presence on the island.

"This is your room, I believe." Nick opened a door, revealing a large room with thick pale green carpeting and walls painted a pale buttercup. The bedroom pieces were white, trimmed with touches of gold, Gena noted in amazement, almost identical to the antique furniture that filled her own room back in New York. Before she could comment on this, a second sense warned her that she and Nick were no longer alone. She saw him stiffen as he gazed steadily past her. Gena automatically turned, meeting the cold, black eyes of Alexander Andreas. Her breath almost stopped.

As he continued toward them, her pulse began to pound. Without being conscious of it, her left hand let go of the leather purse strap slung over her shoulder and crept protectively toward the throbbing pulse in her neck. She wanted to swallow, but her mouth was dry. Her legs felt like rubber, ready to bend.

Everything about him was dark. His deeply tanned, chiselled features fairly shouted his disdain for her, despite his own disreputable garb, which consisted of a pair of beach thongs, worn jeans, and an open shirt. Gena found herself involuntarily intrigued by his image, a distinct contrast to the well-dressed man she had seen every now and then in the newspapers. He came to a dead stop just a few feet from where she and Nick waited, cupping his hands to light a small, thin cigar. A gold signet ring caught the bright flicker of flame. The air was heavy with tension as he replaced the lighter in the pocket of his snug denims. His jet eyes flickered down the length of her. Gena tried not to stare back, but her own gaze was unwillingly drawn to the curling black hairs that ran down the center of his chest. His white shirt, unbuttoned and dotted with what looked like paint stains, had clearly seen better days. Smoke curled between them. Wasn't he ever going to speak? When he finally did, she wished that he hadn't.

"Just where the hell have you been?" he asked Nick unpleasantly. "You were supposed to be here before Mother took her midmorning rest." His nostrils flared, exhaling smoke.

Nick reacted angrily. "And leave Athens at sunrise?"

Alex's lips tightened.

"We came as soon as we could. Look, can't this

interrogation wait until a little later? I'm sure Gena
doesn't want to hear all the boring details."

"Where's Spiros?" his brother asked. "I didn't
see him exit the copter."

"He didn't come."

"You know perfectly well I told you never to
travel without him!" Alex snapped, his six-foot
frame stiff with rage.

Who was Spiros, Gena wondered, a bodyguard?
She shifted her weight nervously. Should she slip
into her room and let them continue their verbal
battle in private? She was startled when one of
Nick's arms drew her to his side.

He ignored his brother completely for a moment,
saying to her, "I want to check on Mother. If she's
awake, I'll tell her you've arrived." And then to
Alex, in a cool tone, "In case you don't know it, this
is our niece, Gena. The least you could do is greet
her with civility. After all, you haven't seen her
since she was a little girl, since Ava died."

Gena forced a smile.

"You don't have to tell me who she is, Nick, nor
do I need you to remind me of my manners," Alex
warned as Nick turned to leave them.

There was a small, uncomfortable silence after
the younger Andreas son rounded a corner and
disappeared from view.

Gena cleared her throat lightly. "Nick's been
very pleasant to me since my arrival." Her voice
sounded husky to her own ears, and she wished
desperately that she was safely behind the door of
her room so that she could gather her wits. "If you

don't mind, I'll go freshen up so that I'll be ready to
see Grandmother."

Alex nodded curtly. "When you're ready, come
to my study and I'll take you to see her. It's across
from the music room. Do you know where that is?"

"Yes. Mother used to play the piano for me and
sometimes strum a bouzouki, if there was one
around. . . ." Her voice trailed off as she became
suddenly aware that she was on dangerous ground.
Why had she brought that up? His face was without
emotion, revealing none of his thoughts, she saw
gratefully.

"I'll be in my study."

He left her then. She shut her bedroom door
weakly and sank down on a corner of the embroidered coverlet. He frightened her! He was worse
than she had ever imagined. No wonder her father
spoke so bitterly of his encounters with him.

On shaking legs, she moved toward the beautiful
white dressing table. After unpacking a few necessi-
ties she began to unpin her hair, brushing it smooth
as silk.

What was she letting herself in for? She felt
panicky. There was something about him. . . .

"Stop it!" she hissed. She was thoroughly disgusted with her inability to control her emotions.

She took a white sundress from her suitcase; its
color complimented her tanned limbs. Before
changing into it, however, she investigated the
connecting bathroom and blotted a damp facecloth
over her forehead and neck in an effort to revive
her usually calm demeanor. She quickly tied a

matching white ribbon at the back of her neck to hold back her heavy dark hair and left the room, still feeling unprepared for her coming encounter with Alex.

Even before she tapped on the half-open door, Alex's low voice called out to her, telling her to enter.

She saw that his back was to her; he was gazing out the window behind his desk. From where she stood, Gena could see that it offered a spectacular view of the open sea.

"Close the door and have a seat. We have a few minutes to wait." He added, by way of explanation, "Mother's nurse is attending to her, giving her medication. By now I am sure she knows you are here."

"Yes. Nick did say he would tell her," Gena mentioned politely, settling her slim frame into the chair farthest from his desk. She took a deep breath. This is what it must feel like to be in the eye of a hurricane. The calm before the storm.

She glanced around the room. It was a man's room. Somber wood. Books. Strong, well-built furniture. It smelled faintly of his cigar smoke. There were paintings on two of the walls. She recognized one artist's work. The painting's value was beyond six figures.

He still had his back to her. Even if he disliked her, couldn't he at least behave in a polite manner, and say something . . . anything?

As if sensing her feelings, he slowly turned, but

she wasn't prepared for what faced her. For even in the room's muted shadows, the fury in his narrowed coal-black eyes shocked Gena to her very soul.

"I want you off this island in two days time," he said. "Make any excuse you want to my mother, but that is your time limit." His voice rose. "Do you understand?"

"But . . . you asked me to come," she protested weakly. "You can't be serious." Her nails dug into the chair's armrests. The muscles in his jaw moved as she spoke, intimidating her. His nostrils flared; she wanted to cry out. "You can't expect me to do what you ask." Her voice was a mere whisper.

"You will do as I *say.*"

Gena opened her mouth, but no sound came out. A sob rose in her throat. Finally, she attempted, "You can't order me out. Grandmother invited me here. Lots of times. This is *her* home."

His approach was unhurried, but there was menace in his step.

He looks like a panther stalking its prey, she thought wildly. The black pants and shirt which he was now wearing only intensified her imaginings. That she should actually notice his state of dress caused a hysterical laugh to catch in her throat, but it was squelched almost at once by her fear of him. She closed her eyes, trying to gather her wits. They flew open when she felt him cruelly jerk her chin.

Her lips parted with a low cry.

"You dare to give me orders?"

Her whole body trembled. "Please. You're

hurting me," she moaned. She dared not look him squarely in the face; her eyes were close to over-flowing.

He uttered a disgusted sound, then released his hold on her and walked away. Her backbone went limp. She felt like a rag doll. How could she have ever hoped to stand up to this . . . this devil?

At the moment he was half-sitting on his desk, calmly lighting another cheroot. She wished he'd choke on it.

Their eyes met, and it was as if he knew what she was thinking.

Gena fidgeted, and looked away.

A full minute passed, and during that time his eyes never left her. Gena looked up and away again, confused.

She lowered her eyes, not courageous enough to meet the expression on his shadowed face or to try and guess the meaning behind the cruel glint reflected in his cold eyes.

What would happen now? she wondered. To what lengths would he go if she once again dared to protest his order to leave the island? Would he attempt to strike her? She would scream if he laid a hand on her. Nick would hear her and come running to help. She sighed. Her imagination was running wild; she really must get hold of herself.

When a slight movement caught her attention, she gave him a quick look, only to see him tapping hot ashes from his cigar into an ashtray next to his phone. As he bent to crush the cheroot, a narrow band of sunlight danced onto her right shoulder.

She determinedly ignored the annoying warmth, instead concentrating on maintaining what was left of her waning composure, and at the same time fervently hoping that she would survive this confrontation.

A sudden knock resounded from the other side of the study door, its sharp sound interrupting the intensifying silence. Without meaning to, her eyes automatically swung to his face, seeking his reaction to the obvious demand for entrance.

At his command, a short, plump woman entered, carrying a silver luncheon tray. On it were coffee cups, a pot gently steaming with hot coffee and a generous plate of temptingly thin sandwiches, plus a separate dish filled to overflowing with dessert pastries. The older woman nodded shyly to Gena, then murmured a few words to Alex in Greek.

He answered her, smiling faintly as he directed her to place the tray on his desktop. She left them then, making sure to pull the door snugly shut. They were alone again.

"Mother's housekeeper," he offered by way of explanation, while pouring coffee into the china cups. She noticed that he added sugar to only one. This was the cup he handed to her, not bothering to ask whether she preferred it that way or not.

His superior, all-knowing attitude rankled, and as if sensing her underlying irritation, he told her bluntly, "You would find our coffee much too strong."

She said nothing, even shaking her head mutely at his offer of food. Her stomach was quivering madly. How could she eat? She took a small sip of her drink, secretly hoping that it would revitalize her and prepare her for whatever horrible ordeal she was to face.

His matter-of-fact tone cut through her musings, bringing her thoughts sharply back into the present.

"I shall personally arrange for your transport and see you to the airport on Tuesday—to see that you depart safely, of course."

His meaning could not have been more clear. She seethed with resentment, carefully setting down her coffee cup and its saucer on a polished wooden table.

"This is . . . ridiculous. I told you before that I'm here at Grandmother's invitation. My presence here has nothing whatsoever to do with you *or* your phone call of yesterday morning." She spoke with much more assurance than she actually felt; her heart was pounding. "I will not be bullied into leaving."

His expression stopped her from saying anything more. "You will do as you are told, like it or not." He folded his arms across the broad expanse of his chest, his gaze fixed on her anxious face. "Just for the record, I would like to know why you have finally decided to honor us with your holy presence after an entire decade has passed by. Tell me."

His sarcastic tone cut through her, melting her last shred of self-confidence. After some hesitation, she said, "I felt it was time."

"Time! Time for what?" he condemned. "To ply your charms on an old woman? What are you hoping for—a generous share in her will?" He waved an angry fist, then slammed his hand down on the desk, making the dishes rattle alarmingly. "For you to benefit from this . . . sham . . . this pretense, there would be no use in your coming here if the end result weren't measured in cold cash." He was livid. "So don't lie to me, you cunning little . . ."

Gena felt sick. "How dare you talk to me like that?" she seethed. She was on her feet now, both hands clenched into tight fists at her sides, as if she were readying herself for combat. All her energies were focused on him. She was not aware of the cooling, damp perspiration beading in the hollows of her slender throat, nor did she feel it when a tiny rivulet trickled lazily toward the vee between her heaving breasts, which were visibly straining against the once-modest elasticized bodice of her sundress as her breathing deepened.

"How dare I?" he asked arrogantly, pointing a steady finger in her direction, as he moved closer to her. "I have a normally suspicious nature. *I know more about you than you think.*"

Her bravado disintegrated. His sinister words seemed to carry an added, hidden meaning. He knows. He's known all along that I'm not really who I claim to be . . . that I don't really belong in his family circle. A sob rose in her throat.

She would have crumpled into a heap if he hadn't reached her in time, pushing her none too gently back into her chair.

Tears blurred her vision. She was beaten. There

was no more fight left in her. He had won. Hands down, he had won. Her chin trembled so that she couldn't speak for a moment. She pressed a hand to her waist, very much aware that he was watching her every movement.

Her brain reeled. She sniffed, feeling sorry for herself. "Oh, heavens . . . how I wish I'd never . . ."

"Go on," he encouraged.

Gena folded her hands in her lap, their knuckles showing white.

"It was such a shock. I first found out about . . . two weeks ago. My life just turned upside down . . . all in the space of a few minutes." She shook her head in misery. "I never dreamed . . ." Her words trailed off into a whisper.

There was a minute of silence. "You have only known for a few weeks, you say?" His dark brows knit together, his eyes distant.

She nodded, brushing an escaping tear from her right cheek.

His mouth tightened. "You shouldn't have been allowed to come here."

"Father wasn't in favor of it," she admitted. "He was very much concerned what your attitude would be if . . . if you knew my circumstances."

He digested this last bit of information. She heard him curse under his breath.

"You won't say anything to Mother?"

"Of course not!" she gasped, her violet eyes fluttering in shock.

"I have your word on this?"

"I wouldn't dream of telling her," she declared, outraged at his question.

"Have you told my brother?" he persisted grimly.

"Why . . . no. After all, it's not something I care to broadcast." She was becoming genuinely puzzled by his line of questioning. "Unless you want me to tell him . . . ?"

His contemptuous glance raked her. "If I were to allow you to stay for any length of time, you would be forced to . . ."

Gena's forehead puckered. She opened her mouth to ask him just exactly what he meant by his last remark when a buzzer went off on his desk. He bent toward the telephone.

From where she sat, Gena could hear the caller, though she could not understand their conversation. She noticed that Alex's face had softened, its hard, angry lines melting into a half-smile as he spoke quickly in Greek. Gena felt left out. Her mother had never bothered to teach her her native language. A pity. Because right now she was dying to know what was being said.

When he finished his conversation, he explained, "That was Miss Vouzas, Mother's nurse. Mother is waiting for us." His eyes were like steel chips again, she noticed. Her hopes plummeted. For a few seconds, she had almost believed him to be human!

Surprisingly, he waited politely for her by the door and opened it. She walked by him, head high. At that same instant, a streak of red came barrelling around a corner, crashing fullspeed into Gena, throwing her off balance. It was Ana, of course, Gena realized as she swayed backward, at the same time reaching for the little girl so that she wouldn't fall and hurt herself. Gena, in turn, found herself steadied by a pair of warm, strong hands that encircled her waist.

She quickly righted herself and moved away from him, covering her breathless confusion by smiling down at the dark-haired six-year-old who was curiously appraising her.

"Are you Gena?" Her brown eyes widened as she spoke.

"Yes. And you must be my cousin, Ana." At last, a friendly countenance, she thought. Then she watched in dismay as Ana's mouth turned down.

"But . . . you're so big! Almost as big as my papa," she said in obvious disappointment.

"Ana! Your manners," her father admonished sharply, still standing close behind Gena.

The youngster was not to be mollified. She sniffed unhappily. "I hoped she would be little, like me, so that we could play together."

Gena smiled at this and dropped to her knees to give Ana a hug. "I was your size once, but even though I'm much taller now, I still love to make sand castles and find pretty rocks and shells. Would you like to come down to the beach with me later?" she asked. "You know, when I was a little girl, just like you, I loved playing on that very beach. I learned to swim here."

"You did? Could you teach me while you're

here?" She looked behind Gena to her father, saying half-accusingly, "When Papa takes me to the beach, all he ever does is lie on a blanket and watch me play. He's no fun at all!"

Gena managed to suppress a giggle. Children were known for their honesty and Ana was no exception.

"Ana, that is enough of your chatter! It must be your lunch time now. Off with you. I am sure Eleni is waiting for you in the kitchen. Gena and I are on our way to see your Grandmama."

After her father had spoken, Ana bobbed her dark curls submissively, while Gena got to her feet, helped in part by one of Alex's hands under an elbow. Ana said her goodbyes and left them, scampering toward the kitchen.

"Stand still a moment."

"What?" she turned, startled by his strange request.

"Your hair ribbon has come undone. Let me fix it for you so that we can be off to Mother's room."

She automatically put a hand to her hair, self-consciously aware that she must look a mess. She felt her hair curve loosely around her shoulders as the ribbon dropped, slipping out of its proper place. It felt heavy on her bare skin. She was almost thankful when she felt him grasp the first handful to lift it so that the satiny band could be placed underneath once more. His hand brushed her bare back. She stared straight ahead, trying not to let his nearness affect her.

"Ana speaks English very well," she began brightly.

"She should. She had an English nanny up until last year," he replied. "There. All fixed. Let's be on our way, or Mother will begin to worry." He looked her over critically from head to toe. "Couldn't you have worn something a little less revealing?" He pursed his lips. "It's too late to change now." He shrugged and pressed a hand at the back of her waist, to hurry her on.

Twin spots of color rose in her cheeks because of his last remark, but she willed herself to remain silent. It would do no good to start another argument with him now.

2

~∞∞∞∞∞∞∞∞~

Maria Andreas held out both arms to Gena, who stood hesitantly in the doorway.

"My Gena," she crooned in a frail voice.

Gena was shocked at the changes the years had wrought in her grandmother. She hurried to her, her own eyes brimming with tears as she laid her head gently on the older woman's shoulder, which was supported by several pillows. The fragile arms held her fiercely for a moment before they relaxed somewhat. "Such a long, long time, my sweet baby." She smoothed Gena's dark hair. "Child . . . child you shake so."

With an imperious wave, she ordered the nurse and Alex from the room. "If I die now, I die happy. Leave us. Yes, even you, nurse. I want some time alone with my grandchild."

After the two of them had dutifully filed out, Gena slipped off the bed, kneeling by it instead. Her grandmother continued to smooth her hair back from her face in a soothing gesture, much as she had done years before.

"Ah, if only my Ava was with you again. But you and I, we will be happy, yes? Your mother would be pleased. Gena, dear girl, you cry so. What is it?"

"I'm so . . . glad to see you again," she gulped. Yet she knew her sobs were more than just for her happiness at this precious reunion. Her chin quivered. The pleasure was bittersweet.

"Come. Stand up, so that I can take a better look at you."

Gena did as she was told, first hastily wiping her tears away with the backs of her hands.

"Ahh, yes." The old woman's pride was evident in her voice. "You are a beauty. You look like a film star, my dear." The dark eyes grew sharp. "You are still a virgin, yes?"

Gena's mouth dropped open at the forthright question, but she eventually nodded an affirmative. She could feel her cheeks grow hot.

"I congratulate your father, then. He has raised you well." She patted a spot at the edge of her bed. "Come, sit next to me. There, that's better," she said, closing her eyes for a moment. "I tire so easily these days." She reopened her eyes, smiling wanly. "You came quickly. I am so happy to have you here with me again. I am content." She appeared to be in deep thought, or on the edge of sleep. Then, to Gena's surprise, she announced, almost gaily,

"What you need is a good Greek husband. I will have Alexander invite one or two of his unmarried friends over to meet you. . . ."

Gena grew alarmed. "Grandmother . . . no, please. That's not necessary."

"Kostas, I think, would be perfect for you. He is a little old, maybe, but he is rich." She was not even listening to Gena's protests.

"Grandmother, I'm not ready for marriage."

"Pah! All I ask is that you meet an acquaintance of my son's. You would not deny an old, dying woman her last wish?"

"Actually, there is someone special back in New York," she fibbed, panicking at the thought of meeting any marriage prospects.

"You are betrothed?"

"Not . . . exactly."

"What is the name, please," the matriarch commanded.

"Ah . . . Robert. Robert Collins," she invented.

"I can tell by your face that this is not the man for you." Her expression took on a faraway look. "When your dear mama spoke of her James . . . I knew." She was silent for a moment. Then, "I had hoped to see both my sons settled before I die. I fear that Nick will never marry after seeing his brother's marriage come apart. You would not have known about that." She stopped speaking to take a sip of water. "Alex met his wife in Paris; she was a singer. He married her and brought her back here to live until a proper home was built near

Athens. She left him when Ana was two years old. Alexander was in England, on business. When he returned home it was to find his little daughter being cared for by their housekeeper." She sighed softly. "A month later, Helene's car was found. It had run off a bridge near the Spanish coast. She did not survive."

"How terrible." Perhaps that was why Alex was so bitter, partly so, anyway.

"Yes. It was a bad time. I hope that he will marry again. Ana needs a mother. I am no longer able to spend time with her, other than short visits. My end is near."

Gena's eyes blurred. "Please . . . please don't talk like that. Won't you consider going to Athens, at least for a complete check-up?"

"Leave my island?" Her head moved from side to side. "Never!"

"But . . . if I came with you, stayed with you as much as I could, would you go then?" She had spoken impulsively, but she watched with growing excitement as the older woman appeared to be seriously weighing her proposition. "I could visit you every day," she added, persuasively.

"If I agree to this operation the doctors told me of, would you also return here with me while I recover, that is, if the surgery goes well?"

"I would," she answered promptly, uncaring what Alex would think of her promise.

"You are a good child, Gena." Her wrinkled hand trembled as she gently squeezed Gena's slender one. "I . . . I will think about it," she sighed, tiredly.

"Oh, Grandmother!" She was ecstatic.

"I must sleep now, my dear. There has been so much excitement today." Her eyelids drooped.

As Gena tiptoed from the room, she found only Miss Vouzas stationed outside the door. She had half-expected to find Nick, too. His voice had reached her ears a while before, and she had so wanted to share the good news with him.

The petite nurse smiled at her, then quietly told her, "They have gone to . . . the beach. Ana had Eleni make a . . . a picnic lunch in honor of your . . . arrival. You are to . . . to change into swim clothes . . . and join them." Her English was pleasantly accented, though she sometimes hesitated, as if unsure of her words.

Gena laughed softly. "Ana is making sure that I keep my promises. Thank you for telling me, Miss Vouzas."

"You are most welcome, Miss Fielding."

As she turned to go, Gena pleaded, "Won't you call me Gena?"

The young woman agreed. "And I am Dimitra," she whispered over her shoulder, pushing open the door to her patient's room.

Upon entering her bedroom, Gena noticed at once that all her clothes had been neatly hung in the closet and that the drapes had been drawn against the sun, which was now high in the sky. There was a brisk breeze blowing through the open window, filling the room with warm, fresh scents. Gena began to undress, quickly stripping down to her lacy underwear, and with the utmost speed began opening dresser drawers looking for the two swimsuits she had brought. She found them, together with the white, thigh-length terry wrap that she used as a beach jacket.

She immediately opted for the less revealing, deep purple one-piece suit, and slipped into it. But after she had adjusted it, she hesitated, bothered by the fact that it was cut quite low in the back. She went to stand before the dresser mirror, to take a better look.

"Oh no!" she moaned, half-covering her eyes. It wasn't the back of the suit that she had to worry about, after all. The front, though cut in a vee, had seemed rather modest when she had tried it on at the store, especially in contrast to the bikini she had also bought at the time. But now . . . She swallowed hard. It wasn't so much the cut, as the material. It was made of a smooth, stretchy material that clung, outlining every contour of her well-developed figure. It looked almost . . . brazen. Every movement she made drew attention to her high, full breasts, taut against the fabric. Even her legs looked barer and longer.

Her eyes sought the brief, two-piece suit that lay on the bedspread. She threw her hands up in disgust and grabbed for the beach jacket, flinging it on and tying it securely at her waist. She had pinned her hair up haphazardly just before trying on the swimsuit and she decided to leave it that way. In one hand she clutched her beach thongs, and in the other her sunglasses. It would feel good to get into the water, she thought. A trickle of perspiration was slowly making its way down the center of her back.

Ana was the first to catch sight of her. She waved excitedly, watching as Gena made her way down the steep, rocky path to the hot sand.

A giant beach umbrella shielded Nick, who sat sipping a beer, comfortably positioned on a colorful blanket spread out on the clean white sand. Just as she pushed her sunglasses on, she saw him turn and she waved, hurrying to tell him the hopeful news about his mother's change of mood. Her lips curved in a smile.

"Nick! I have the most fantastic news!" It was then that she noticed the other pair of muscular, tanned legs. Alex was there, too, stretched out on his back, arms covering his face, seemingly asleep. Her own shapely legs turned to rubber.

"Then tell us!" Nick called as she approached them. He smiled at her lazily, admiring her leggy appearance.

"It's about Grandmother," she began breathlessly. "She promised me that she would consider going to Athens. . . ."

"Gena! How did you do it?" he demanded at once. He bent her down to kiss her soundly on her rosy cheek. "You sweet angel!" Then he turned to his reclining brother. "Alex, did you hear?"

Gena could see that he wasn't sleeping, as she

had supposed. "I heard. Tell us how you managed it."

It was a command.

Gena nervously pushed her sunglasses higher on the bridge of her nose, then sank to her knees on the blanket before replying. Ana, she saw, was playing in the shadow of the cliff, out of the sun's hot rays.

"I merely told her that I would stay with her as much as I possibly could, that I would find a place to live in Athens while she was in the hospital. And . . ." She heard Alex make an angry sound under his breath. "And," she continued, "she then asked me if I would be willing to return here with her until she was recovered. That's when she said she would consider going to Athens. . . ." She stopped, out of breath but triumphant.

Alex sat up. "That might take months. . . ." He reached for his cheroot case. "How can you stay here that long?" he asked, with a piercing look.

"Under the circumstances, my father won't mind." She tried to look innocent.

"I am not thinking of your father. . . ." he ground out pointedly. His hooded gaze made her feel uncomfortable. It seemed to say "cheat . . . conniver. . . ."

"Alex, what's wrong with you?" Nick asked impatiently. He scrambled to his feet. "Gena's performed a miracle and instead of thanking her, you're questioning her about her length of stay, even after she's assured us that she can and will remain! Come on, Gena, let's have a swim before we have lunch. Ana's paddling in the water now. Let's go join her."

It would be a pleasure just to get away from Alex's prodding. But she was very self-conscious about her appearance . . . and with Alex waiting and watching . . . She bit her lip. What should she do? If she stayed on the blanket, Alex would return to questioning her. No way, she thought, would she go through that, not after the session in his study. She just wasn't up to another grilling. So, off with the beach jacket.

With shaky fingers she unlooped the sash, turned her back to him and dropped the white garment behind her on the edge of the blanket. She was about to join Nick and Ana, who were gleefully splashing each other, when Alex's hard voice ordered her back.

"Just one moment." Her feet stilled. "Get back here and sit down. I don't know what kind of game you're playing, but we're going to have this out once and for all."

She turned slightly, not facing him. "I came here to swim, not to have another big dramatic discussion."

"If you don't turn around and sit down, I'll get to my feet and make you."

His threat, she felt, was not an idle one. Gena, shivering, even though she was standing in the sunlight, at last turned sulkily to walk the few feet back to where he waited under the shade of the striped umbrella. She steadied herself after dropping to her knees once again, mentally preparing herself for his scrutiny.

"*Christos!* If you were my daughter, I would have put you in a convent!" his words lashed. "You might as well be naked!"

Gena's cheeks blazed with color. She made herself push a lock of fallen hair back on top of her head as if she were unconcerned with his condemning words. "Just what did you want to discuss?" she asked pointedly.

"I want to know how you are going to manage it. Have you thought of that . . . in your condition? Providing I allow you to stay," he added grimly.

She looked at him directly, her expression perplexed. "I'm not ill. I am a very healthy person. I don't *have* a 'condition.'"

"Don't be obtuse!" A hand raked his dark, ruffled hair in irritation. "Earlier, in my study, you revealed that you had recently found something out . . ."

"Yes . . . ?" She turned her head to smile at Nick and Ana as they yelled to her in unison, urging her to come and join their fun. Ana was sitting on Nick's broad shoulders, screeching and giggling, her face screwed up in a show of delight.

"Pay attention!"

"You told me you knew everything. What more is there to say?" Her tone was flippant. "I can't help what happened," she added, while waving at the two who beckoned to her.

"You can't help . . ." He gave her a long look,

then barely moving his lips, he tersely asked, "Are you or are you not pregnant?"

She caught him in the jaw with one wildly swinging fist. Her left hand struck out, too, but he caught it just as it descended toward his hair-roughened chest. Before long, he held both of her wrists captive.

"By your response I can only hope that I was wrong," he ground out, looking into her blazing, tearful eyes. "Just don't ever hit me again or you'll wish to heaven you'd never been born!" He thrust her away. "Now go and get wet before my daughter and your Uncle Nick start howling for you again. Don't think I'm finished with you. I'll be seeing you after dinner this evening. Something isn't right and I mean to find out what it is. Make no mistake, Gena, you had better be prepared to tell the truth." He got to his feet and strode off in the direction of the house.

Her troubled gaze followed him. It was obvious that he knew nothing about her adoption. He had been bluffing, pretending. . . . Well, she was either going to have to tell him the truth or leave. The latter was really no option. She was on an island. She would have to be truthful, unless . . . unless she could convince him that she really *was* pregnant, as he had been so willing to believe. No. It wouldn't work. Knowing Alex's suspicious nature, he would probably insist that she visit a physician, and she would be right back where she started. Also, she wouldn't put it past him to demand the father's name, even going so far as to contact her own father in New York to corroborate the story. There were too many drawbacks, not the least of which was that she might be in Greece for a good length of time. But, would he actually believe the truth, preposterous as *that* sounded? Only time would tell.

Nick's shout put a stop to any more deep thoughts on the matter. "Gena," he called, "why are you sitting there like one of our ancient statues? Come join us."

The three of them eventually lunched in the cool shade of the rocky overhang, then spent several lazy hours enjoying one another's company. When the afternoon was on the wane, they returned to the villa where Gena excused herself to shower and have a rest before the evening meal. She knew she would need all her strength for her after-dinner encounter with Alex.

When she awakened, the drapes were once again being whipped about by a breeze bearing the fresh pine scent of the island, deliciously caressing her bare shoulders and face as she lay covered only by a silky sheet. She stretched, at the same time idly listening to the muted sounds of the household. Finally, after several more minutes had passed, she managed to rouse herself. Nick had mentioned the fact that they would be dining at eight o'clock. She had an hour in which to put on her makeup and dress.

The question was, what would she wear? Should

she don her "gypsy dress," as she called it? The saleslady had admiringly spoken of it as a sexy peasant type, whatever that had meant. Anyway, the description had made her laugh. It was in actuality a chic, off-the-shoulder, "little black dress" with tiers of dramatic ruffles at the hemline. But she made a face and placed it back in the closet. It just wouldn't do for tonight. Instead, she drew out a classically styled cream silk. It was very plain with a rounded neckline and an elasticized waist that fit her like a dream. Pearl buttons ran from neckline to hem, a few inches below her knees. She had bought it on sale on an expedition to Seventh Avenue, where one could often buy designer clothes for less than half-price.

After she finished dressing, she headed toward her grandmother's suite, but when she found the right door and nudged it open, she saw that the nurse was having her meal and her patient was asleep. Gena left them undisturbed.

To her surprise, there was no one in the dining area on her arrival. And the table had been set for only two. As she was puzzling over this, Alex appeared in a doorway, his tall frame nearly filling it. He glanced at her coolly, then made for the liquor cabinet, mixing himself a drink.

"Where are Nick and Ana? Aren't they having dinner?" She stood with her back to the patio doors, watching him.

"Nick took off in the copter about two hours ago. Ana just had her dinner in the nursery wing."

"You planned it this way," she said, quiveringly.

"And if I did?"

His tone was incredibly arrogant. How could she ever hope to converse with him, to explain . . . ? She turned to stare out the window. "Have you spoken with Grandmother yet?"

He inclined his head. "It seems you are to be congratulated. She has agreed to fly to Athens in two days time, providing, of course, that you come along. If she has surgery . . ."

Gena whirled around. "What do you mean, if . . . ?"

"The doctors might decide that the odds are worse if she has an operation; she is rather weak, after all."

"I . . . I see." She moved to stand under a small chandelier, the light spilling over her coiled dark hair and her bare arms. She ran a finger over the polished wooden dinner table that graced the center of the elegantly furnished dining room.

"Could I have a drink, please?" Her voice sounded jerky; his statement had shaken her.

He handed her a glass filled with a delicious dry red wine. "It's Greek. It will go well with your dinner."

The eldest of Eleni's two teenage daughters served them their meal; the main course was succulent roast lamb, with a variety of side dishes that were impossible to resist. Gena chose to finish her meal with baklava, a dessert pastry partly made up of nuts soaked in honey, and coffee, while Alex lit one of his cigars and poured himself an after-dinner brandy, thoughtfully leaning back against the chair's silken upholstery.

"Would you care to take a walk?" he asked her, finally breaking the silence that had lasted through the meal.

Her answer was to rise. She needed to clear her head; the wine had left her sleepy.

"It would seem that you employ an entire family here," she commented politely as they moved toward the open patio doors only a few yards away.

"Yes, we do. Yanis and Eleni's three sons also live here. They patrol the island, do repair work, and so on." He pointed to the east. "They have been staying on my yacht this past month instead of in their parents' cottage. Just around that rocky point lies a natural harbor, the perfect shelter for my boat."

He followed at her heels, watching as she cautiously stepped off the flat gray rocks and onto the sandy path. She noted in surprise that the sea was barely visible from this side of the house because of the banks of trees and the rolling hills.

"Why did Nick go to Athens?" There. It was out. The question had been on her mind all through dinner. She would have appreciated his presence tonight.

When a crisp shirtsleeve brushed her elbow, she took a quick step to put a little more distance between them.

"Because he has business to attend to, of course."

"Of course." But her tone was disbelieving.

A bruising hand clamped down on one of her wrists, halting her progress. "I will not put up with such insolence," he warned her.

The fierce look he bestowed on her made her think twice about trying to pull free.

"When I came to dinner this evening, I had made up my mind to be pleasant, even tolerant, but your attitude shows me that you are determined to initiate bad feelings and provoke me, which, in turn, will only make things more difficult for *you*. So be it." He flung her hand away and strode back to the stone-flagged terrace.

"Don't go blaming me for your bad temper," she called to his receding back, at the same time smoothing back several strands of her wind-tossed dark hair. "Or for any other flaws in your character. You enjoy making people miserable—me in particular!" She stamped her foot for emphasis. "So don't bother denying it!" He didn't, which made her all the more furious.

To calm herself, she faced the breeze, letting its coolness wash over her hot cheeks. The sun was almost gone. There was no place to go but back to the villa.

He was waiting for her in the shadows of the dining room, the glowing tip of his cigar warning her of his presence as she stepped through the heavy glass doors.

"Come with me."

Gena stiffened at his brusque tone, but she didn't dare resist his command.

* * *

"Well? Out with it."

They were back in his den. One small lamp glowed from a far wall, throwing almost frightening shadows onto both ceiling and walls. Gena half-expected him to tip its small dark green shade, aiming its arc of brightness on her features. She bit her lip; she must try to still her wild imaginings. He was waiting for her to begin . . . watching her with an intentness that made her extremely nervous. The brunt of his weight was taken up by the desk, his arms folded across his chest. At least he wasn't dressed in black anymore. He looked like the devil himself in black. . . . The tailored slacks he wore tonight were of an expensive-looking gray material, the shirt a lighter pearl gray that had a silky sheen to it. She watched numbly as he approached her.

"Don't stall. You know what I'm talking about!"

Her head whirled. "Would you like a shortened version, or a little more for your money?" she asked carelessly, unable to stand the tension. She was at the point of screaming.

"Damn you . . ." His voice cracked like a whip.

She put a hand up as if to ward him off. "All right. I'll . . . tell you." Her nostrils quivered. "But . . . first would you mind . . . er . . . sitting *behind* your desk in . . . your chair?"

He looked at her, his question unspoken.

"That way," she explained shakily, "if you decide to take drastic measures, I just might make it to the door first." She smiled weakly.

His words were almost gentle, surprising her. "I

have no intention of hurting you. Now tell me what has been troubling you, Gena. I give you my word . . . my word as your mother's brother . . . that I . . ."

"But that's just it . . ." she broke in, wildly. She looked up at him, her violet eyes wide with anguish. "You aren't really . . . my . . . uncle!" A shuddering breath escaped her and she covered her trembling lips with cold fingertips. "We aren't related—not at all."

"Kindly explain that extraordinary statement," he demanded.

It took her a moment to gather more courage.

"I'm not the daughter of your sister . . . and . . . and . . ." She stopped after hearing him draw a sharp breath. She forced herself to go on. "I was adopted."

"Tell me about it," he said roughly. "Is this what's been bothering you . . . the thing you discovered just lately?"

"Yes."

She kept her head down so that he wouldn't notice the tears spilling down her cheeks. Even when several rolled off her chin and dropped onto the front of her dress, she made no movement to wipe her eyes. She heard him sigh and before too long a spotless fine linen handkerchief was thrust into her icy hands.

"You must know that what you've just told me isn't true. . . . Your father lied to you. Ava was with child . . ."

Gena sobbed all the more. "You . . . don't

under . . . stand," she gasped. "I was switched. And she never knew. . . ."

He grabbed her roughly by the shoulders, dragging her to her feet, all the while muttering under his breath. "I'll have his neck for this! Is he mad?" And then to Gena, he said grimly, "Stop torturing yourself . . . I tell you Ava was pregnant . . . I saw her myself some months before when she flew here for a visit!"

"You still don't . . . understand," she moaned, leaning her aching forehead against his shirt front, near his pounding heart. "I was switched. . . ."

"You said that before!" he shouted, giving her a shake. "What on earth are you talking about?" He pushed her away slightly, so that he could see her face. He felt her knees buckling and at once would have set her back down in her chair, but she clung to him, needing comfort. His hard body was rock solid, a fortress. She dug her hands into his back, its muscle rippling as he helped her maintain her balance.

"Their real baby daughter died . . . almost immediately after she was born. I was substituted," she croaked in a voice that sounded strange to her own ears. "My natural mother, you see, was . . . wasn't married. I'm . . . illegit . . ."

He crushed her face to his chest, muffling the last of the condemning word.

"It's incredible. An incredible story . . . but somehow I feel that I must believe you."

Her muscles hurt from trying to control her sobbing. It was almost a full minute before she could bring herself to move away from him, groping in back of her for her chair, where she sat to finish her story. She told him all the details, including how she herself had found out.

"Father's been wanting to tell me for years, but he . . . he didn't know how . . . or when. . . ." she ended, her emotions spent. "Please . . . if you don't mind, I'd like to go to my room now."

She undressed in the dark, tossing her clothes onto a chair, then crawled into bed after pulling on a short nightie. She had no energy left to take down her hair or wash her makeup off. She didn't feel like even looking at herself in the mirror . . . her face felt puffy and blotched from all her crying. With a deep sigh, she put a hand to her aching forehead, reliving some of the more embarassing moments. Why, oh, why hadn't she been able to just tell him everything in a matter-of-fact way? But no, instead she had fallen apart at the seams—it was the only description that fit.

It didn't take much imagination to figure out what his ultimate action would be. He would send her packing. She didn't belong here anymore—in any sense. A nonentity, that's what she was. Her thoughts were bitter. She drew a deep, shuddering breath, squeezing her swollen eyelids shut to hold back the tears that threatened again.

"He knew nothing . . . Gena, you're such a dope," she whispered, berating her stupidity. And now everything was spoiled—her trip, her visit with Grandmother.

An alarming thought entered her brain. *What*

would happen to her father? Would Alex banish him, make him leave the shipping office? She tossed about the bed in a worried state. She would have to warn her father somehow.

"*Must* warn him . . ." she muttered, her lashes fluttering downward.

3

~∽∾∿∾∿∾∿∾∾~

She saw no sign of Alex the next morning as she wandered about the villa after breakfasting on coffee and rolls on the sunny patio. When Ana found her later, in the music room, curled up in a chair reading, the little girl begged Gena to take her to the beach so that they could begin her swimming lessons. Gena donned her white bikini this time, and they swam and played until just before lunch, returning in time for Gena to visit with her grandmother before the light midday meal was served.

She dined alone that evening, as Ana had again been served an earlier meal, and Dimitra Vouzas preferred to remain near her patient—as had been her practice during the month she had been on the island.

"Where is Mr. Andreas?" Gena finally asked the shy, pretty girl who had just placed a delicious-looking bowl of fish stew on the crisp linen place-mat laid out in front of her.

"He . . . the master . . . is on . . . the boat with my . . . brothers," she responded in her hesitant English. She made an explanatory motion with her hands. "They . . . take the paint . . . off."

When she had gone back into the kitchen, Gena sighed discontentedly. Even though her grand-mother had assured her that Alex would be in charge of all their arrangements and that she was not to worry, Gena couldn't help but feel appre-hensive. She wasn't too sure of anything after last night. Uncertainty had gnawed at her all day. She felt like she was walking a tightrope. Fleetingly, she wondered if Alex was deliberately avoiding her. Her position in the household was a precarious one. She contemplated this while buttering a warm, crusty roll. If he ordered her off the island, there wouldn't be much she could do. But would he risk it, knowing his mother needed her at least until after the operation . . . ?

Just as she was about to leave the table, a door slammed. She felt ridiculously nervous, knowing it must be Alex, hearing footsteps approaching the dining room.

It was not difficult to tell that he had been working. He looked tired and dirty and paint stains were streaked across his faded jeans. His shirt was open to the waist, the sleeves rolled past his elbows.

A few sprinkles of white paint clung to his dark stubble of beard.

He had stopped a few feet from her, his thumbs hooked carelessly in the back pockets of his pants. "I thought you would have finished by now."

Gena drew in a steadying breath. This was not the time to get angry. "I have. And you?" She scraped back her chair to get up after seeing him shake his head in a negative manner.

"I'll tell Eleni . . ."

"No."

She looked at him curiously.

"Don't trouble yourself," he said wearily. A grimace of pain escaped him. He shifted his weight to the other foot.

"Before I leave you—since you obviously want to be alone—I should like some information. . . ."

"Well? What is it?" he asked in an irritated tone.

"I just wondered if I'm still needed in Athens, and if so, where will I be living?" She was still sitting and she felt at a disadvantage. "I don't know if it's possible to find a hotel room at the height of the tourist season, unless it's booked quite far in advance . . ." She busied herself setting her silverware onto her dinner plate, finally getting to her feet after doing so.

His eyes seemed to bore into her. "Since Mother's trip hinges on your attendance . . . yes, of course you'll be needed. And as to the other question, there is no problem. You will be living at my apartment in Kifissia."

"Oh . . ." she breathed. It was the only thing she could think of. She hadn't even thought of staying there.

"Which reminds me," he continued, rubbing the back of his neck at the same time, "I hope you can cook and straighten up after yourself. My housekeeper is visiting her daughter on Corfu. I gave her time off since I had planned on being here for quite some time."

"I'm not helpless," she said, her eyes flashing.

"Good. You'll be on your own most of the time, since Nick has his own place. There are guards; you don't have to worry on that score. You'll be safe there." His look revealed nothing as he went on, "My nights will be spent . . . elsewhere." He paused. "You will have a driver available whenever you wish to go to the hospital or shop."

"Thank you," she said coolly. "What time do we leave in the morning?"

"Be ready at nine. Nick and a . . . friend of mine are flying in with a copter capable of carrying the six of us very comfortably. If you have slacks, wear them."

"When it's hot," she began deliberately, "I prefer wearing skirts or shorts."

"You'll do as you're told! I'll have enough on my mind tomorrow without worrying about whether or not you're properly clothed."

Their warring eyes clashed.

"I wore a skirt when Nick brought me here, so I'll wear what I please on my return trip." And with that, she picked up her dirty dishes and marched toward the kitchen door, her long, freshly-shampooed hair swirling loose and silky around her shoulders and down her back.

Eleni looked up in astonishment from the table in the center of the well-equipped cooking area, for just after Gena burst in, she was followed by a glowering Alex. Gena nervously deposited the dishes she held onto a countertop by the sink.

"That was delicious, Eleni. Thank you."

"And you may serve my meal in one half hour," Alex cut in smoothly, his voice coming over her left shoulder. "And now," he addressed Gena, "if you are on your way to wish my mother a good night, I will accompany you, however filthy I look."

"Actually, I . . ." She got no further.

"Good. Let us go." He steered her toward the door.

They were barely through the entranceway when she hissed, "I saw her before. She's asleep now."

"You know very well that I said that merely as an excuse to get you out of the kitchen." He gave her a raking glance. "You will wear slacks tomorrow, do you hear? And do something with that hair of yours, too. Put it up, or tie it back."

"Yes, Uncle Alex," she simpered in an overly sweet tone. After hearing the curse he muttered under his breath, she was at once sorry for her rash words. "I'm sorry, it just slipped out."

"If you *ever* use that tone of voice with me again, I'll make you pay. Believe me." He rubbed the back of his neck again. "You *can* call me Alex. After all, you're on a first-name basis with my brother.

Let's not stand here sparring any longer. We have a busy day ahead."

She hesitated before leaving him. "You *do* believe me . . . about my adoption, don't you?"

His nod was brief. "I will require absolute proof, of course. I am going to contact your father. I want to be very sure. . . ." He broke off. "Look. Would you do me a favor, and forget all our antagonisms for a few minutes?"

Gena looked at him curiously. What could he possibly want of her? Her hands nervously clutched the pale green of her dirndl skirt.

"Would you give me a neck rub? I have the most awful kink."

Gena didn't know what to say.

"Well?"

"I couldn't."

"Why not, for heaven's sake?" He sounded annoyed again.

"I . . . I'm tired," she answered lamely, backing away a step. "Besides, I'm on my way to bed now."

"You look almost frightened." His alert eyes roved over her pale features, noting the startled, doe-like quality in her shimmering look. "Are you afraid of me?" he demanded. When she did not respond immediately, he walked past her, saying, "I'm sorry I asked. . . ."

When she caught up to him, he was almost at his own door.

"Alex, wait!" She was a little short of breath when she reached his side in the dim hallway.

"If . . . if you still want me to, I'll massage your neck. I'll be glad to help. You just took me by surprise, that's all."

"Forget it," his low voice commanded. "I'll stand under the shower instead." His hand was already turning the doorknob to his bedroom. "Or perhaps I shall ask Dimitra for a rubdown."

"But, really," Gena pursued, "I . . . I wouldn't mind." She was unaccountably shocked at the thought of him asking the nurse to engage in such an intimate-sounding activity—at this time of the day.

He gave her a long, level look, a strange, feverish look that made his eyes almost glow. "Well, *I would.*"

Gena could see that every movement of his neck and shoulders was causing him to suffer. She circled around behind him, deciding to ignore his remark. He tensed when he felt her hands press into his back, but when her efforts began to ease his pain, she was pleased to hear his first pleasurable groans. She stayed on the surface of his soft cotton shirt for a time, but then, without even thinking about it, she pushed its collar aside, allowing her slender fingers to mingle in the crisp dark hairs that grew at the nape of his neck.

With a sudden jolt, she realized how much satisfaction it was giving her to touch him, to make him feel good, to feel his damp, warm skin beneath her hands, and to be close enough to smell the strong, musky scent of his body. While she pondered this alarming response, her hands lost some of their energetic force, slowing down to a more sensual pace. She resisted the almost overwhelming desire to draw herself up against him, to wrap her arms around his chest and cling to his back. Panic swamped her. She retraced her steps and faced him, her heart pounding.

The thing to do was to politely excuse herself and go to her room, two doors down from where they stood. Once there, she could sit quietly for a while and try to evaluate the strange, new emotions that were raging through her body.

His eyes were closed, she noticed at once. He looked so totally relaxed with one hand braced on his bedroom door that she hated to disturb him. Gena pressed a hand to her heart, then raised it, lightly touching his forehead and temples, applying a soothing motion with first one hand, then with both. When her aching arms faltered after a minute, she was unable to stop them from sinking to his bare chest, her trembling fingers spreading out on his muscled, tan flesh. He spoke then.

"Don't stop." His eyes lifted to reveal a slumberous longing. The hooded, steady gaze seemed to drink in the shadows near her unsure, startled eyes, her flushed cheeks, and the shocked parting of her mouth, moist where the tip of her tongue had touched it.

"I . . . I . . ." What had she been going to say? It didn't matter. Nothing mattered.

"Gena . . ."

Gena's entire body shivered when he extended a hand to smooth back the fine, dark hairs that grew by her temple. His hypnotic touch rooted her to the spot.

A breathtakingly sensual outline of her face came next, his exploration ending when he trailed a thumb over the bridge of her nose to brush her parted, trembling lips.

Was that *her* strange-sounding cry, she wondered dizzily? Her eyelids felt strangely heavy, as did the lower half of her body. She barely had the strength to stand. She swayed toward him, in part held up by her palms resting against his chest.

He seemed particularly fascinated with her mouth; his thumb continued to rub its pink softness. Though it made her breathing difficult, she found the resistance to compress her lips in an effort to thwart his intimate caress. He smiled faintly at this maneuver. Then without warning, he pulled her close, pressing unbelievably light, feathery kisses along her jawline and throat, his other hand dropping to unbutton her gauze shirt, under which she wore only a lacy bra, its shade of pale green exactly matching the color of her skirt.

When she felt the blouse being pulled out of her waistband, alarm raced through her. She started to move away, but a hand stilled her. For the first time in her life a man's hand lay on her breast.

"You . . . we . . . mustn't . . ." she panted. But she was forced to stop speaking as his mouth claimed hers, halting the rest of her protestations. Their breaths mingled as he explored her mouth, his tongue tasting, thrusting . . .

She did not have the will to resist when he

half-carried her the rest of the way into his room and closed the door, propping her up against it. With a suddenness that stunned her, the wispy light green lace was pulled adrift and his strong fingers began to stroke and tease an exposed nipple. Gena arched her back against this assault, but her reaction only seemed to give him greater pleasure because he moaned with satisfaction against her lips. She couldn't stand much more of this. . . . When he began to fondle her other breast, her agitation increased. She lay a hot cheek against the cool wood of the door, accidentally causing a swirl of silky hair to fall over her left shoulder and the bare flesh his hand was caressing while his lips trailed kisses of fire down the exposed column of her neck.

She gasped as he probed through the mass of hair, searching with his mouth until he was able to find and sample the tip of her other breast, nipping her lightly when she attempted to pull away.

Her hands grasped the back of his head, urging his lips to meet hers once more. She willingly followed his hoarse instructions when he ordered her to take off her skirt. When it had dropped to the carpet, he gripped the elastic waist of her half slip with feverish intent.

But as the slim band of elastic reached the fullest part of her hips, his hands suddenly stilled. A knock penetrated the thick wood at Gena's back, startling them both. Gena's eyes widened, assuming a combined look of guilt and fear, overriding the blazing passion of an instant ago. She felt Alex press a hand to her waist, his touch warning her to remain quiet, not to panic. She complied, slowly releasing a quivering breath, a little at a time. Dimly, she heard Alex demand in a low, hoarse voice, "Who is it?" By this time he had drawn himself up to his full height, and when he felt her shiver nervously, he began to lightly stroke her throat, as if to calm her. His attention was focused on the door, his other hand was now placed firmly against the polished wood, to the right of her head.

After hearing Eleni's muffled Greek tones address Alex, Gena's knees buckled and she sank to the thick carpeting, leaning her forehead onto one of Alex's knees where the denim was worn soft and smooth. Dawning shame mixed with her cooling ardor, and a little bit of fear as well—fear of this strange, arrogant man who had awakened such primitive stirrings in her. She was vulnerable in her confusion, and was totally unprepared for his complete about-face.

"Get up and get dressed!" He jerked his leg away from her, turning his back. With hazy eyes, she watched him fling his balled up shirt onto the dark blue spread that covered his bed, then disappear to turn his shower on. Still, she continued to sit, curling her fingers into the deep pile of the blue-patterned rug. When he reappeared to find her still in his bedroom, he reacted angrily.

"What if Eleni returns? I told her I had drowsed off, but that I would have my dinner shortly. Would you like her to see you sitting half-naked on the floor, or worse yet—he paused meaningfully, cocking his head at the bed that did not fail to dominate the generous-sized room, "find me tangled in the covers with . . . *my niece?*

"I'm . . . not . . ." she protested, her voice a shade above a whisper. With an effort she began to reassemble her clothes.

He bit out a curse, irritated by her incomprehension. "I know you're not and you know it . . . but as far as anyone else is concerned, I am still your uncle!" He threw his belt on the bed, then began to lower the zipper on his jeans. "There is no lock on that door. If it weren't for the fact that Mother might be told if we were discovered . . ." He groaned. "I tell you, Gena, I am not cut out to be a celibate . . . and it has been over a month since I have had a woman. . . . Do you understand? Now you know why I was so susceptible to your fancy little massage out in the hall. . . . Just get out of here, will you? My bathroom door *does* have a lock, if you get my meaning."

His speech left her feeling numb, sick. The truth behind his blunt words was just beginning to sink into her system. Yet she found herself unable to look away from him as he began to slide his jeans down his lean hips, now clad only in clinging black trunks. It didn't seem to bother him that she should stare; then she deliberately turned her face away in embarrassment, fumbling with the row of tiny buttons on her blouse.

His laugh was cruel. "Don't pretend you've

never seen a man undress before. Your response a while ago certainly proved that."

Once back inside her own room, she sat numbly on the bed. Her head whirled sickeningly and her stomach churned. She felt used. Cheap. Dirty.

Her body . . . that was all he had wanted. She made a funny sound in her throat, wanting to cry. What was wrong with her? She let her hands drop to her lap, raising her head. Maybe a bath would help. At least she would be clean. Just then her eyes lit on the bikini that lay in a soggy lump at the bottom of the sunken marble tub.

A swim, she thought, that would be even better.

The moon was up, spreading its silvery glow over the entire island, lighting the path so that she had no trouble making her way down to the shore. The breeze from the sea seemed to have a calming effect on her. Even her head hurt less.

She came to stand at the water's edge, straining her eyes to gaze out over the vastness of the ebony sea before wading in. When it reached her thighs, she stopped, clamping her even, white teeth together to stop their chattering.

Her forehead creased. What was that? She shrugged, then dove into the water, the sound of the whispering waves soon muffling all else. Her slender, pale arms cut cleanly through the foam at first, but her legs soon began to drag and her arms grew heavy as she fought the spirited waves which pounded into her, physically draining what little energy she had left. Then, surprisingly, the water grew calm. She had enough sense to turn and float on her back to conserve her strength. She managed to paddle every now and then so that she wouldn't be sucked back into the shore's rushing surf.

Just when she thought she would attempt the return trip to solid land, her body tipped and water seeped into her mouth, causing her to choke and cough. Her legs felt like lead. She submerged, but by some miracle, she found her head back above water, and she cried Alex's name . . . again and again.

She was so tired. The wetness gently settled over her again. This time she could offer no resistance.

Suddenly she kicked at the water, flailing her arms madly. Something hard had hurled itself at her. She made a valiant attempt to struggle from its reach, though her motions were slowed by the weight of the water. Her lungs. They needed . . .

Air!

She gulped in the precious element, at the same time struggling against the force that held her head above water. She raised a hand to her hair in an effort to release the pressure that held her a prisoner. She began to shriek.

"Gena! Stop it. It's me . . . Alex. There now, don't fight me," he coaxed. "Relax. Let me take you in."

"You . . . can't be . . . Alex," she choked, keeping her eyes tightly shut. She could barely move her lips.

"Look at me. Feel me." He grabbed one of her hands and pressed it to his mouth and throat.

"I'm afraid. I . . . it must be you, but . . ." She coughed, driving the water from her lungs.

"What do I have to do—make love to you to prove it?" he joked, though his eyes were devoid of humor. He continually moved his legs, keeping them afloat.

"Gena," he commanded.

But her eyes remained closed as he stroked strongly for the shore, ever careful to keep her head above the water. He carried her onto the beach and laid her carefully down, holding her face in his lean, strong hands and calling softly to her.

When he spoke her name, she raised her head weakly, then dropped it back onto the wet, gritty sand. She was on her side, facing him. She curled up, sobbing.

"Why . . . didn't you . . . just leave me . . . there?" she wailed.

She was silent as he made the steep climb, with her in his arms, until he grunted in pain as his ankle turned on a loose rock.

"Please. Put me . . . down," she whispered unsteadily. "I can . . . walk."

"No." His tone of voice did not encourage an argument.

The warm bath water had the desired effect. She stirred under his intent stare.

"Care to tell me about it?" He knelt by the tub,

71

waiting. "It's a good thing I was passing a window. . . ." One of his fingers twirled in the water near her shoulder, brushing her bikini top. "Why, Gena?"

"I didn't set out to drown myself, you know," she began, her voice like ice. "I needed a swim."

"The devil you did!" He got up off his knees and picked up the facecloth that was hanging on the edge of the tub, throwing it into the water near her.

"You needed a *man!* And don't try to tell me any different." He moved toward the bathroom door. "I'm coming back to check on you just as soon as I change. When you feel thoroughly warmed, get out of the tub, get dressed, and get into bed. Is that clear?"

"Very."

She was combing the snarls out of her hair when he knocked. Her hands shook slightly when he came to stand behind her.

"Are you feeling better now? If not, I can have Miss Vouzas . . ."

"I'm fine," she interrupted, wishing he would go away. "If you don't mind, I'd rather not have anyone else know . . . what happened."

There was a tiny silence.

"Nine o'clock tomorrow, then. Be ready."

"I plan to." She tugged the comb through her hair somewhat recklessly, uttering a low cry as it pulled at a tangle, hurting her scalp.

"Let me help you. You're worn out." He moved to take the comb.

"Don't touch me!" She clutched the neck of her robe. "Please . . . just leave."

He inclined his head. "Good night," he uttered formally.

After Gena heard the shutting of the door, she turned away from the mirror, her face a picture of misery. Did he honestly think she would let him remain in her bedroom and perform such a personal task for her? After what he had put her through?

When she was finally ready for bed, she wearily climbed in, wondering aloud how she would make it through the coming weeks.

Surprisingly enough, she slept soundly and dreamlessly, awakening around seven o'clock as she had hoped. She blinked sleepily once or twice, then rolled over just in time to see her door being pushed open.

"Good morning. I brought you some coffee."

Alex. What was he doing in her room again? He was making this a habit.

"I offered to awaken you. Ana wanted to come, but she has the beginnings of a cold," he said brusquely, offering a cup. "I thought it best that she remain quarantined until Mother is safely on the copter." He drew a breath, watching her fluff up her pillow, her breasts taut against the thin fabric of her nightgown. "How are you?" he asked tonelessly.

"Fine. And you?" she asked coolly, accepting the cup.

He ignored her question. "I spoke with Mother. She seems to be in good spirits."

Gena smiled. "Good. I'm going to stop by and see her before we leave."

"Do that. Kostas and Nick won't be arriving until almost nine. That will give you plenty of time." He turned at the door to face her.

"Kostas?" she murmured. "I believe Grandmother . . ."

"Go on . . . you were saying?"

"She intends to play matchmaker. Didn't you know? She's picked Kostas to marry me." Gena sipped her drink calmly. "She wants a great-grandchild."

Alex regarded her coldly. "There isn't a woman born who could get Kostas Stavos to the altar. He's far older than I am—and ten times as cynical about women."

Gena kept her expression bland. She raised a shoulder, careful to keep the slippery sheets tucked under her upper arms. "I must say, it would be a challenge, but she seems to think he's ready to settle down. . . ."

"If you're in the market for a husband, return to the States. Given half the chance, Kostas will bed you, Gena. But marriage? Never!"

"Well, I have one thing in my favor, so we shall see."

"And what might that be? Your youth, your beauty?" He shook his head, laughing drily. "You are not the only female with such visible attributes. Beautiful young women are a dime a dozen to someone as rich as Kostas."

"I'm sure that's true," she admitted and, aching to bait him, to make him show something, went on, "but how many of those beautiful, available women can claim that they have never been with a man—in the most intimate sense?"

He raised a dark brow.

"You don't believe me?"

"What you are saying is that you are still virtuous." His black eyes glinted dangerously. "I came very close to taking you last night, Gena. Do you really think that I would have allowed myself to lose control if I even suspected that you were still a virgin? Besides, it is difficult to coach an untried girl in the art of pleasing—something I certainly did not have to do with you last night."

What was he talking about? she thought dazedly. All she had done was stand there, holding him. Before she could protest, he went on, "I'm warning you right now not to hint at such a thing to Kostas. If, by some remote chance, he did place a ring on your finger, only to find out that you are a fraud, heaven help you!"

"How dramatic you sound." She forced a smile. "I promise you that Kostas would be pleased, much as you think otherwise, *Uncle Alex!*" She shivered after he had gone. The look on his face . . . Why had she taunted him like that? She owed him her life. Her head turned to one side and a tear slid out onto the embroidered pillowcase. And she hadn't even thanked him for saving her, dragging her through the deep, unfriendly waters, carrying her back to the villa . . . And yet . . . it had been because of him that she had nearly died.

"Oh, I don't know . . . I don't know anything anymore," she moaned, kicking back the covers. In a matter of a few days she had turned from a healthy, well-adjusted young woman into a miserable, unsure neurotic! And it was all because of *him!*

4

~eeeeeeeeeeeee~

There. She was packed and ready. She could easily eat breakfast and stop by her grandmother's room for a brief visit before it was time to leave.

As she walked past the oval mirror on the dressing table, she caught a quick glimpse of the floral-patterned voile skirt and blouse she wore. The matched ensemble made her look and feel chic. The thin, silky material was fashioned with green and blue embroidered flowers on a black background, its vibrant colors complementing her dark hair and creamy tan, at the same time reflecting a startling mix of lavender-blue in her sooty-fringed eyes. High-heeled sandals, their thin, black straps encircling her slim ankles, complimented the mid-calf length of her skirt. She had chosen to pull back her hair, clasping it with an enamelled black barrette at the back of her head so that her fragile, shell-like ears were exposed, drawing attention to the small, gold hoops she had donned. Her only other adornment was an antique gold watch from her father.

She pivoted, her eyes sweeping the room. On top of the carry-all bag near her suitcases lay her slim leather purse, its color exactly matching the dull gleam of her shoes. Safely tucked inside it was a letter to her father. She must get Nick to post it for her so that she could warn her father that Alex would soon be contacting him . . . that is, if he hadn't already. The unnerving thought made her tighten her hold on the doorknob. Her mind raced. Surely Alex's flat had a phone. She could easily place a call to New York this very evening. Alex need never know about it. . . .

She breakfasted on the sun-splashed patio, then hurried to chat with her grandmother. Just as they greeted one another, the increasingly steady drone of an approaching aircraft invaded the room, breaking the peaceful sounds of the island's natural environment.

Gena squeezed the veined hand that curled around a corner of a pale-colored sheet.

"You will be near me in the days ahead, my dear?"

"Every moment, if you want," she promised quietly, feeling the slight tremor course through the pale hand that lay under hers. "But don't forget

that Dimitra, your nurse, will be by your side, too."
Gena's glance took in the serious young woman
who was deftly preparing her patient's medication
for the trip.

"Yes. She is a good girl . . . a fine nurse."

"Those sweet words will not excuse you from
taking these two tablets, Madame!" the white-
uniformed woman teased smartly, though she softened her brisk words with a lovely smile.

"Go now, dear one, and send my youngest son
to me." Her tired eyes twinkled at the nurse's quick
humor.

"Of course, Grandmother," Gena murmured,
dropping a light kiss on her nearest cheek.

"And Gena . . ." The older woman paused expectantly. "Our pilot is to be Kostas."

"So I heard." Her reply was smooth.

"It is good that you wear a dress. It will make a
good impression. So many young women wear
nothing but jeans. Pah!" She shook her head
vigorously, waving one of her frail-looking hands.
"That is not the way to interest a man. . . ."

Gena bit her tongue to keep from telling her that
she had no intention of "interesting" this Kostas
. . . whoever he was, even though she had hinted
to Alex that it would be a challenge to do so.

Masculine voices filtered up from the main salon.
An uneasy feeling overtook her. Alex would certainly not be pleased with her choice in clothes,
even if his mother was. With a tiny sigh and a shrug,
she stepped onto the thick wool carpeting that
graced the floor of the living room, only to feel a

curious disappointment when she saw that Alex was not present.

"There she is!"

Gena couldn't help but smile in response to Nick's enthusiastic greeting.

"Gena, you are looking even more beautiful than before, if that is possible." The boyishly smiling Nick turned to address the casually dressed man standing next to him.

"What did I tell you, Kostas? Isn't she a rare beauty?"

A crimson flush spread over Gena's cheeks. "Nick, *please*," she whispered. She had never considered herself beautiful.

But before her lashes fluttered down she glanced up at the other man. Kostas was very handsome— in a very Greek way, she thought. He was almost her height, as she stood in her heels, and he appeared to be tan and fit. A luxuriant, but well-trimmed moustache decorated the space above his upper lip. It was dark, as dark as his thick hair. There was no sign of gray in his hair, despite his age—which Gena knew to be in the mid-forties.

Nick draped a casual arm around her waist. "Kostas, meet my niece, Gena Fielding. Gena— our friend, Kostas Stavos."

"I'm happy to meet you, Gena," the man said in a cultured, barely accented baritone. "Nick has constantly sung your praises since we left Athens this morning." He bowed slightly. "I can only say that I agree completely with everything he said."

"Mr. Stavos, you're too kind, really." She

laughed lightly to cover her confusion. And because she could think of nothing else to say, she stated, "I . . . I have been told that you are to be our pilot today."

"Unfortunately, yes," he drawled, while his coal-black eyes looked directly into her startled violet ones. Seeing her look of surprise and puzzlement, he drew even closer to her, his face a few inches from hers, completely ignoring Nick's presence. "You see, if I were a passenger, we could become better acquainted." His teeth gleamed. "But since I must fly the craft, I fear we must wait until Athens before getting to know one another on a more intimate basis."

"You . . . you're overwhelming me, Mr. Stavos," she gasped, unconsciously laying a shaky hand to her throat. Here was another man who didn't beat around the bush. She felt Nick's hand bite into her waist.

"You must begin by calling me Kostas. Say it." His tone was persuasive.

"Kostas," she breathed with docility.

"Very good." He patted her cheek. "We are going to get along very well." He turned his attention to Nick, who was watching them with wary eyes. "I am sure you must have something you must attend to, Nickolas?"

Gena pressed guilty fingers to her lips. "Oh, Nick. I nearly forgot! Grandmother wants to see you. I just came from her room."

"I will wait. Alex will be here in a moment." His mouth was set in a stubborn line.

Kostas Stavos frowned. "Am I not to be trusted alone with your niece, hmm? What are we—children?" He was clearly offended.

Alex walked in and it seemed to Gena that Nick actually breathed easier.

Alex gave his brother a sharp look. "Mother is asking for you," he said coldly. "We should be leaving in half an hour." His eyes fell on Gena, who was standing between the two men and he addressed her in the same tone. "I had your luggage put on board. Your handbag is still on your bed, however."

"Thank you." She nodded slightly, determined not to allow his grim stare to upset her.

"Eleni is about to serve coffee and cake. Let us move into the dining room."

Nick disengaged his arm, stepping away from Gena to talk with Alex. When Kostas politely offered his arm, there was nothing she could do but accept it and walk with him into the adjoining room.

"I really shouldn't have any," she announced brightly. "I had my breakfast not too long ago." Her name floated back to her from Nick's flurry of Greek. She could just imagine what was being said. . . .

Kostas gave a hearty laugh at her faint protest. "You need not worry about your figure; it is without fault. One more roll and some coffee will not ruin it!"

Alex took his seat directly across from Gena and Kostas, but she didn't dare look across at him.

"Please, Mr. Stavos." A fleeting look into Kostas'

face convinced her that he was being deliberately mischievous. He seemed bent on provoking Alex.

When his warm fingers splayed over her own, where they rested on her lap, she tensed, staring straight ahead at the low floral arrangement that graced the center of the table.

"But it is my pleasure to speak to you thus, Gena. You color so delightfully." His breath rustled the few strands of hair that had escaped her barrette, as he whispered, "And my name is Kostas —remember?"

She jumped, gasping softly, when Alex's fist hit the fine white tablecloth.

"*What do you think you're doing?* Are you feeling well, Kostas?" he snapped, as he rose from his chair and circled the table to where Gena sat. Without warning, he grabbed her by her forearm. She got to her feet willingly, without protest, ridiculously glad when Alex pushed her into a chair next to his.

"I never felt better. What is *your* problem, old friend?" the other man questioned. "Could it be that you are upset because I am showing your beautiful niece some attention? I assure you, my intentions are strictly honorable."

Eleni's sudden presence did not deter Kostas from speaking. As she began to pour their coffee, Kostas rubbed his chin thoughtfully. "You are so very protective, Alex, that if I didn't know you and your family, I would swear that she was your daughter. Or," he shrugged, "your woman."

Gena sat as if petrified.

Kostas calmly stirred his coffee. "But then, I can only suppose that part of your vexation is due to worry about your mother." His mouth split in a taunting grin. "And perhaps you miss Sofia, yes?"

Out of the corner of her eye, Gena could see one of Alex's hands clench into a fist.

"I offered to keep Sofia warm while you were gone, but she refused my kind offer. Alas, I managed only to take her out to dinner a few times. She would not even set foot in my new house, though I told her I needed her expert advice on how to decorate it." Kostas shook his head, lifting his cup to his mouth. "Perhaps your charming niece will help me in this matter, hmm Gena?"

"No!" Alex began explosively, then calmed himself. "I will not have any more of such talk."

As the two men eyed each other, Gena forced herself to drink some of the fragrant, strong brew. Thanks to Kostas, she now knew that Alex had a mistress in Athens, a mistress named Sofia. Her coffee cup wobbled slightly as she replaced it in its china saucer. Why was she so surprised . . . so shocked? The fact was, he was a man. He had even hinted at the fact, telling her that he was not accustomed to leading a celibate life.

Through eyes that were misty, she saw Nick enter the room. He hurried to sit next to her. "Such silence. Did you run out of conversation?"

"Alex is not pleased with me, I fear," Kostas explained.

Nick's dark brows rose a fraction.

"I made a *faux pas*. Though I told your brother

that my intentions concerning your niece are honorable, he dragged the poor girl around the table to sit next to him. Also," he added, a gleam appearing in his eyes, "Alex does not think it seemly that I mention Sofia in the presence of Gena." He shifted his gaze to Alex. "Ah, yes. I could tell that you were not pleased. But unfortunately, Sofia does not exactly hide in the woodwork. What are you going to do about that, my friend? Rumors have it that she is at your apartment more than she is at her own. . . ."

Gena could stand no more. "Excuse me. I haven't said goodbye to Ana yet." Before any of them could get to their feet, she had left the table. She hurried from the room as fast as she could, short of actually running. To get control of her emotions, she ducked into her own bedroom. She gulped back a sob. So what if Alex kept a mistress? It shouldn't matter to her. What kind of a "friend" was Kostas, anyway? And why had Alex allowed him to say such things?

"Oh, Alex," she moaned brokenly. To suspect that she had been a stand-in for just any woman had been bad enough. Now that she knew the woman's name, it seemed all the worse.

After bending to pick up the slim black purse from the bedspread, Gena quickly unsnapped its rounded leather flap and drew out a tissue, carefully eliminating any traces of tears from her lower lids. She had just seated herself at her dressing table to apply a light dusting of powder to her nose when the door opened. Her heart pounded madly when she saw Alex's tall, masculine form step into the room. He shut the door with an almost imperceptible sound.

"What . . . do you want?" she asked, her voice quavering.

"I stopped by to tell you that we are leaving in about fifteen minutes or so," he announced, coming up close behind her. "I had a feeling that you would not be going to my daughter's room at once."

"Oh, but I was . . . just going there." She started to rise. "I won't be long." She felt his hard fingers close around her upper arms, exerting pressure so that she was pushed back down onto the fragile, cushioned chair.

"You're hurting me," she protested.

"Hurting you? I could wring your neck."

The controlled fury in his voice frightened her. She swallowed hard, determined to maintain a calm exterior.

He gave her a little shake. "Now do you see what can happen when you flirt, you silly girl? If I hadn't been just across the table from the two of you, Kostas would have . . ."

"Done the same as you did last night?" She spoke over her shoulder, interrupting him. "I think not. But of course, that's only *my* opinion. I'm sure *you* think I would have allowed him to seduce me right then and there!" she fumed, trying to escape his hold. "All he did was place his hand over mine and whisper in my ear."

"You were frightened, but of course you won't

admit it." His voice was dry. Then he gave a sigh of
irritation. "Will you sit still? I won't release you until
I'm good and ready." Their eyes met in the mirror
—his angry and serious, hers rebellious.

"I would not care to speculate as to the number
of women Kostas has bedded, but I'm going to do
my best to see that you don't end up among their
ranks!"

"How kind of you."

He drew in a steadying breath. "I am also going
to ignore your innate nastiness for the moment," he
began, "because I have something else I wish to
discuss with you." His hold on her loosened and he
began to massage her bruised arms, sending
pleasurable tingles down her spine.

"What happened between us last night," he
announced calmly, "is probably worrying you. But
it shouldn't. It was a spontaneous, physical act
which will never occur again."

"But if I hadn't . . ."

"It wasn't your fault!" he exclaimed harshly,
giving her another shake. *"I* should have been the
one with more control. . . . Once you had aroused
me, all I could think of was my own gratifica-
tion. . . ."

His frank words sent a crimson flush to her
cheekbones. He stood tall again. "I want to apologize. I said some cruel, uncalled for things. But I was
half out of my head . . . furious with myself, angry
because Eleni interrupted us. . . ." His voice grew
husky. "I also half-convinced myself that I despised
you for giving yourself so . . . freely, so sweet-

ly. . . . Then I came to my senses. Eleni had gone and you were sitting half-naked on the rug, clinging to my leg, your face flushed, your eyes enormous with fear. I wanted you even then. . . ."

"You didn't want me. Any woman would have done," she lashed out at him. She jumped to her feet and faced him. "But don't worry, Alex. We'll be in Athens soon, and undoubtedly Sofia will be waiting with open arms . . . in bed!" Gena watched his face turn a dull red. Recklessly, she went on, "Or isn't one woman enough for you? Possibly you have mistresses dotted all over the city. You can jump from one bed to the next. . . ."

"Stop it," he ground out. "You're becoming hysterical."

She gulped back a sob. "Well how do you expect me to act? You're in my bedroom every five minutes, it seems . . ." She turned her back to him so that he wouldn't be able to see the misery on her face.

"Believe me, this is the last time I will ever enter your room, unless it is by direct invitation, and since we will be living in separate residences for the next few weeks, I think that will be highly unlikely. Before I go, however, I'll warn you again. Stay clear of Kostas." He paused. "Perhaps if I tell a little story about him, *then* you will be convinced. Do you know why Kostas is here today? He still feels guilty. Yes. Every now and again his conscience bothers him."

Gena turned around, curious. "Why?"

"Because my wife was infatuated with him, and he kept her at a distance just so long, if you get my meaning."

"But how do you know that she and he . . . ?"

"Helene and I had begun living separate lives after Ana was born," he stated, ignoring her gasp of surprise. "Kostas was not her first lover. I never questioned her comings and goings, as long as she was discreet—nor did she inquire into my personal matters."

"But . . . you could be wrong!"

"About my wife and . . . ? No." He shook his head. "The private investigator was a professional. I have photos and . . ."

Gena's next words were bitter. "You probably had her watched all her married life! If so, I can see why she turned to other men."

"Why you little . . . !"

Gena cried out as his hands shot out to grab her. In the next instant, however, his arms dropped back to his sides. He was breathing heavily.

"Fortunately for you, time is short. We're leaving in a very few minutes." As his hand turned the white and gold enamelled doorknob, he turned and informed her, "I spoke with your father late last evening."

Gena's hand crept toward her throat. No use in sending the letter now; what would be would be.

"He is going to send your adoption papers to me today. And by the way, I thought I . . . suggested . . . that you wear slacks?"

She looked at his sardonic expression, speechless.

A moment later, he was gone. She covered her mouth with shaking fingers, unable to think clearly.

She could not refuse Kostas' hand as he stood in the doorway of the silver helicopter, since he had offered Dimitra the same service. She looked around admiringly, pleasantly surprised by the luxurious interior, noticing the wood panelling and the dark red carpeting.

Kostas noticed her interest. "My company builds and equips custom aircraft, such as this," he told her. Then he added slyly, "Perhaps you will allow me to take you on a tour of some of our islands, hmm?"

Gena could not help but smile. "Kostas, you are . . . irrepressible."

His teeth gleamed. "You forgive me for acting so boorishly, then? I tend to forget myself at times and say what I feel," he said, leaning close to her. "Now be a good girl and go strap yourself in. There is a seat next to your Uncle Alex. Do you see how he glowers at us?"

Gena saw, though she had tried not to notice. Then, clutching her handbag, she made her way to her seat, careful not to look into Alex's face. He had left her an aisle seat so she could sit closer to her grandmother's specially rigged cot, bolted to the floor between the seats.

Nick made a thumbs-up sign, indicating to Kostas

that all was in readiness. As the copter's blades began to rotate, Gena tensed, hurriedly trying to secure the lock on her safety belt.

"Do you need some help?" Alex asked, increasing the volume of his voice to rise above the whirling of the blades.

She ignored him, but the catch wasn't working properly. The craft was lifting.

"Here. Let me . . ." He brushed her fingers out of the way and clipped the belt shut, cushioning his left arm against her breast. The brief contact made her shiver, but she kept her eyes resolutely averted, their overly bright gaze trained on Kostas' back.

They had been airborne for less than five minutes when she saw Kostas beckoning to her. She went forward, eager to put distance between Alex and herself.

"I'm lonely up here," he half-shouted, as she took the seat next to his.

They soon began to pass over several rocky, barren-looking islands. Kostas proudly named them all.

"I shall certainly miss this gorgeous blue sea when I return to New York!" she exclaimed. "It's beautiful."

"Why go back?" he wanted to know.

"My father is there. Besides, it's my home—it's where I was born." Her throat tightened at her words. "I shall be staying here only as long as Grandmother feels she needs me."

"Have your father move to Greece," Kostas

suggested at once. "Alex would have no trouble finding someone to fill his position. He has many capable men in his organization."

"My father loves New York." Gena wrinkled her nose. "I don't know if I could get used to all this sunshine, either."

He laughed.

"I'd miss the snarl the city gets in whenever an inch or two of snow falls . . . or a sudden cloudburst in Central Park. Or the fireworks over Manhattan on the Fourth of July. . . ." Her eyes were shining mistily.

"Marry me and we'll keep an apartment there," he said smoothly.

"Kostas! For heaven's sake!" she hissed. "Suppose someone hears you. People don't get married after knowing each other less than an hour."

He flashed her an arrogant look. "I don't follow any set rules." A large pleasure boat came into view below them. "It is Alex's."

Gena looked at him, startled.

"He must plan on using it while he is in Athens."

"Oh, I suppose he will be living on it," Gena put in artlessly.

"Isn't he staying in Kifissia?"

"No. I'm going to be . . ." She clamped her lips together, finally realizing just what he was doing. "Never mind."

He patted her knee, laughing. "Ah, yes. I think it is time that I settled down. I want a family. A son. I am tiring of this endless merry-go-round. I need a wife. Someone I can be proud of, love and respect."

Gena stirred uneasily. It occurred to her that Alex might be able to overhear some of their conversation, even over the steady drone of the motor and the whirling blades. Kostas did not believe in lowering his voice.

"I'm going back to sit by Grandmother," she told him swiftly.

He nodded. "Think of what I said, Gena. I meant it."

His seriousness unsettled her. As she moved to her seat she encountered Alex's stony face. When she slid in next to him, saying nothing, he asked sarcastically, "Well, what is your answer going to be? Are you going to put him out of his misery?"

Gena flushed. "You heard?"

"Do you think I'm deaf?"

She looked about self-consciously, sneaking a glance at her grandmother, then at Dimitra and Nick.

"Don't worry," he drawled. "No one else has paid the slightest attention. My brother and Miss Vouzas have been conversing and Mother is sleeping."

Gena gave him an irritated look. "What I do is none of your business. Whatever you think you overheard, please forget it."

"You're under my protection, Gena," he stated grimly. "I'm making it my business to know where you go and what you do while you're in Athens."

"You just try and boss me, just try it." Her color was high. She was angry. "And then explain to your mother why I returned to New York—unexpectedly!" she hissed with reckless abandon.

"If you ever dare to leave without my permission, you will regret living. Believe me," his voice grated.

"Just a few days ago you couldn't wait to get rid of me."

"That was before you persuaded my mother to enter the hospital, and you know it! If you hadn't, you would be back in the States by now."

His breath rustled a stray strand of hair by her ear. When he shifted in his seat, turning his attention away from her momentarily, the length of his cream pants pressed hard from her thigh to her ankle. She tensed, pulling away. Almost instantly he moved once more, sliding his leg within touching distance of her again.

"What are you trying to do, punish me? All right. I shall keep my promise. But just you stay away from me. And tell that pillow friend—isn't that what they call mistresses here?—to keep to her own place. If she comes fluttering around, I *will* leave!" She stared down at her lap, marveling at her daring. When he didn't respond, she slid a look in his direction. The muscles in his jaw were clenched tightly.

"I . . . I'm sorry," she mumbled.

"You're going to be sorrier than you think," he said, rising from his seat and moving toward the front of the copter.

It wasn't so much a threat as a promise.

Since Alex had gone forward to sit across from Kostas, she had an unobstructed view as the aircraft drew close to the Greek capital. The city's whitewashed buildings, glinting brightly in the noon sunlight, fascinated her. She sighed with pleasure, her nose to the window, on seeing Athens' looming central hill, Mount Lycabettus, coming into view on her right. Its funicular railway was clearly visible, as was the top, the journey's end, the little chapel of St. George.

It was going to be fun exploring Athens, she thought. The city had never been more than a quick stopover for her and her mother on their yearly visit to Greece. Her mother had preferred spending Easter, the most important festival on the Orthodox calendar, on her parent's island, far away from the hubbub of the city.

But now . . . if all went well, she could rise early and do some sightseeing on her own before she spent the day at the hospital.

Soon the helicopter began its descent and she turned toward her resting grandmother, then fastened her eyes on Alex's strong back and tried to prepare herself for their next encounter.

She waited apprehensively for the helicopter blades to cease their noisy circling. Kostas had landed at the hospital heliport, not far from the sprawling, four-story building where her grandmother was registered. Before the blades had made their last revolution, an emergency vehicle had pulled up next to the aircraft to transport its drowsy

95

patient toward the receiving doors. Gena and the others soon followed, walking slowly toward the main entrance.

The hospital was quite modern, with several comfortable waiting areas where visitors and relatives could wait in private. Nick and Gena remained in one such room now, while Alex arranged for his mother's registration in another part of the large complex . . . much to Nick's annoyance.

"We have been here nearly an hour," he chafed, pacing the small, rectangular sitting room.

Gena smiled faintly, looking up from the Greek phrase book that she had been studying. "I'm sure there's a lot of paperwork. . . ."

Nick ran a hand through his thick, wavy black hair. "I only want to know what's going on. . . ."

Gena rose. "I'm going to ask for directions to a ladies room and tidy up." She waved her thin phrase book. "I think I know how to ask." She squeezed his arm. "I won't be long, Nick."

Feeling considerably refreshed, she approached the same door on her way back, only to overhear Nick's stubborn tones. "I refuse," he was saying. "After Mother is settled in for the night, I am expected elsewhere. Gena doesn't need a nanny; she's old enough to look after herself."

She entered then, only to see Alex get to his feet and approach his brother menacingly.

"I couldn't help but hear what Nick said, and I agree with him," she said, her head held high. I am quite capable of looking after myself, so what's the problem?"

Alex spun to face her. "The problem is *you*. And Kostas."

She frowned, crossing her arms in front of her. "I don't think I understand."

"You silly fool! Don't you know that Kostas was listening to our final arrangements just before I got into the ambulance with Mother and Miss Vouzas? He was deliriously happy to know that you'll be staying alone at my apartment in Kifissia." He hooked his thumbs in his belt loops. "And I don't trust him with you."

"I find that ridiculous!" Gena snapped, moving to a nearby sofa. "He told me he wants to . . ." She stopped just in time.

"To marry you? That's not even funny."

Nick cut in, disgusted. "I'm going to leave you two to your argument. Maybe I can see Mother now."

When he had gone, Alex sighed, visibly irritated. "Face facts, Gena. The age of chivalry is dead. Kostas wants you. And I will admit it *sounds* as if he really does want to marry you. . . . But you don't know him. You're such a gullible little fool."

"And *you* are such a gentleman—to remind me of my one mistake!" Her eyes blazed a deep purple.

He bent forward, taking her chin between strong, warm fingers. "I was not referring to *that!*" His eyes stared into hers. "I know some stories about him, if the one I told you isn't enough, that would make your hair stand on end. He's ruthless. If he really does want to marry you, I wouldn't put it past him to seduce you so that you'd *have* to marry him in the end."

He was frightening her. "I don't believe you. . . . I can handle him."

"You couldn't even handle *me* the other night. If Eleni hadn't come, there would have been the devil to pay!"

She looked at him blankly.

"Do I have to spell it out for you?" he asked, releasing her chin. "What do you think would have happened if Eleni had found us in bed?"

Gena looked up at him, wide-eyed, her lips trembling. "But we wouldn't have . . . done anything like that. Not really."

"You're either incredibly naïve or incredibly stupid!" His rough tone dismayed her. "Which," he continued smoothly, "is precisely why I am going to have to stay at my apartment in Kifissia too. I can't trust you . . . or Kostas. You will have nothing to fear from me. . . ."

Gena risked a look at his face. She swallowed hard. "Er . . . how many bedrooms are there?"

"Enough."

"And Sofia?"

"She is no concern of yours," he stated coldly.

"If she's going to be sleeping with you while I'm in that apartment," she remarked, her temper rising, "I would at least like to know beforehand. You're a fine one to talk about *my* behavior!"

"You will hear no strange noises coming from my bedroom. I will take my pleasures elsewhere—at least while you are living there," he voiced silkily. "Satisfied?" He took her silence as compliance. "Good. That is settled then."

She looked at him out of the corner of her eye. "I imagined you would be living on your yacht. Kostas pointed it out to me on our flight."

"I planned on it. But it was not a wasted journey for Eleni's sons. There are always supplies to be brought back to the island." He checked the time on his thin gold wristwatch. "I will see what is keeping my brother. Then we will have our lunch." He walked toward the door.

"Could we eat at an open booth—a meat pie or something?" she put in quickly. "I'm not very hungry. . . ."

"As you wish."

Left alone, Gena picked up a Greek magazine and flipped through its colorful pages. No more than a few minutes had passed when her eyes grew heavy and she dozed, leaning her cheek on the tan loveseat, the magazine still open in her lap.

5

~∞∞∞∞∞∞∞∞∞~

Gena . . ."

She blinked sleepily, hearing her name repeated softly, to find Alex leaning close to her, a faint smile on his lips.

"We can leave now."

"How is Grandmother?" she asked, her speech still slurred from sleep.

Alex bent to pick up the magazine she had been looking at and put it back on the small wooden table, cluttered with other publications.

"She's been examined and X-rayed. If she passes a restful night, she'll have surgery some-time tomorrow," he said softly. "The doctors tell me she has a heart blockage, as they suspected. But it is operable. . . ."

Gena's breath caught. Without thinking, she reached out and hugged him. "That's wonderful!"

His expression grew strained.

Embarrassed by her show of emotion, Gena let her hands slip to his shirt front, then down to her sides.

"I'm sorry . . . it . . . it's just that . . . I was feeling so happy. . . . I know she's not really my grandmother, but . . ." Her lips trembled and she couldn't go on.

"Forget it." He held out an impersonal hand to help her to her feet. "And if I were you, I would revise my thinking. You, your father, and I are the only ones who know the truth about your parentage. As far as I'm concerned, you are my niece. *And* my mother's granddaughter. And I never again want to hear you apologize to me in that manner."

Gena sensed that he was angry. She ran a nervous hand down the back of her skirt to shake out any creases in the light fabric, unknowingly causing the blouse she was wearing to hug the curve of her breasts, pulling the material taut so that the sheer lace of her flesh-toned bra became visible at the strained button closures.

Suddenly, the heel of her shoe turned, her ankle gave way and her knee brushed his leg. She immediately reached out to steady herself by placing her hand on his arm.

She gave an embarrassed little laugh. "I . . . I'm sorry. Again," she stammered lamely.

"Just stay away from me." His words erupted into the quiet room, startling her.

She paled visibly and backed away a step, noting the set look on his face, the way his nostrils flared.

"Don't look at me like that. I won't hurt you," he muttered raggedly. He rubbed a weary hand across his forehead. "I could use some sleep. I'm sorry I snapped at you. I didn't sleep well last night; whenever I dozed off, I would jerk awake, reliving that moment when you were in the water and I saw you go under. It was torture."

His next few words were whispered in Greek, which she didn't understand, though the way he said them sent chills down her spine. She stood before him clutching her purse, looking young and uncertain.

"Perhaps I really should leave . . . I'm sure your life would be much simpler without me." Her eyes lifted to meet his.

"No. We made a bargain," he stated flatly. He glanced at his watch. "We must go now. Nick will stay with Mother until I return."

"Until *we* return," she corrected him, as they moved toward the door.

He shook his head. "Even though you have just slept, you still look exhausted. I'll take you to my apartment to sleep. Mother won't need you this evening."

His stern, strangely tender expression discouraged an argument.

* * *

A uniformed driver awaited them in a black
Mercedes-Benz parked by the curb outside the
hospital. Once they were on their way, Gena
concentrated on the winding streets, noticing almost at once that they were being driven out of the
city's congested thoroughfares and into a more
suburban setting. Some twenty minutes later the
dark car slowed to a stop in front of a handsome-
looking high-rise, its front doors guarded by two
more men in the same somber gray and navy
uniform that the driver wore. A whisper-quiet elevator took them to the top floor, its automatic doors
opening onto an equally silent and empty corridor.

As she preceeded Alex into the plush comfort of
his penthouse apartment, he broke their silence by
apologizing for not having his driver stop at a lunch
counter as she had requested earlier.

"There's plenty of food in the kitchen. Besides, I
doubt if we would have found any booths open.
Most of Athens is resting now; it's the hot time of
day."

"I wasn't really in the mood for crowds of
tourists—or the heat," she confessed, looking
around.

Off the foyer to her left was the main salon. It was
decorated in tones of brown and cream that
blended together in an elegant yet totally livable
style which, she thought, suited Alex. Fat chocolate-
colored silk cushions decorated the curved sofa.
Gena longed to sink into its plump, soft upholstery,
patterned in a muted brown and cream print that

matched the floor-length draperies dramatically sweeping the entire length and breadth of one wall. It was a beautifully furnished room. Several paintings, highlighted on the remaining wall space, added color and depth, as did a green plant or two, and arrangements of freshly cut flowers.

She wasn't sure how long she stood there admiring the room, but she jumped when he touched her arm. She could tell that her reaction angered him, and she mentally rebuked herself for being so childish. As she followed him up the curved open staircase that led, she assumed, to the bedrooms, she said, with forced brightness, "It's very lovely— your apartment, I mean."

"I'm glad you like it," he said almost formally. "But I cannot take the credit. Someone I love very much is responsible for what you see." He turned and waited for her at the top of the last step. "Since I like my privacy, I could not bear the thought of some stranger having a hand in decorating so intimate a thing as my home. I asked someone whose judgment I trust implicitly."

Gena's enthusiasm dulled. It didn't take much imagination to discern who had done the decorating. Hadn't Kostas said that he had invited Sofia to help him beautify his new Athens house? And that she had refused? And why was it suddenly so upsetting to her to think of another woman in Alex's life? In his home?

"Come along," he said somewhat impatiently. "Your suitcases are in your room. If you need the

services of a maid, let me know; otherwise inform
Spiros, your personal driver, if there is anything that
you require." He stopped before a milky-white
door, pushing it open. He motioned for her to enter
ahead of him.

"Can I ask you something?"

He nodded.

"Why aren't there any other people around?
This whole building seems so . . . so empty."

"I own this building and it's new; very few people
live here yet. Perhaps you are afraid of staying here
with me?" His tone was cool again, as if he could
barely hide his anger.

She blanched at his manner. What could be
wrong, she wondered, as she stepped onto the
room's pale lemon carpet. Could it be that he
resented her living here so much?

"If you would rather that I stayed at a hotel . . ."

His reply was cut short by the shrill tones of the
delicate, French-styled phone by her bedside.

Alex nodded, and she hurried to lift the receiver,
then asked who was calling.

"Gena! At last!"

"Kostas?" Her wide eyes met Alex's stony ones.

"Of course. Now tell me, what is your answer?"

Gena pressed a nervous hand to her throat. "To
what?"

He laughed boisterously. "To my proposal, *eros
mou!*"

She moistened her lips and let her gaze slide
away from Alex. "Could you call me . . . later,

Kostas? I'm a little tired. . . ." The man was practically shouting over the wires, and she knew without a doubt that Alex was listening to every word.

"Do not try to put me off, my sweet, for you will not succeed. I am a very persistent man. . . ." There was a small pause. "This time, however, I will do as you wish."

Gena's breath caught; she had dared to glance at Alex again. His shirt was unbuttoned to his waist now. She felt her heart stir at the sight, and she said a quick goodbye to Kostas and replaced the receiver.

"Is he coming over here?"

"No. He'll probably just call later. You heard me talking to him," she reminded him moodily, her color high.

"Oh, there is no doubt that he will call again. He cannot wait to get you into bed!"

Gena whitened. "That was a low thing to say! But just what I would expect from you!" Miserable, she turned her back on him. "If you don't mind, I would like very much to be alone."

A bath helped her nerves, rattled as they were, and after dressing in her dark blue hostess robe she braided her hair in one thick rope down the middle of her back, then went to find the kitchen. There was not a sound in the entire apartment other than her slippers padding down the carpeted stairs as she made her way down to the first floor. Obviously, Alex had gone back into Athens and she could finally relax.

In no time at all, she had put coffee on, and sliced bread for the toaster. While the coffee brewed, she whipped up two eggs in a bowl, added a little milk, some seasonings, and in no time at all, she was eating a delicious omelet.

When she was sipping the last of her coffee, she heard unmistakable footsteps approaching the kitchen. She waited, elbows on the heavy oak table. It had to be Alex. Luckily she faced the entrance.

"I thought you had gone back to the hospital," she said a little nervously.

"I showered and decided to rest for a while." He advanced, leaning his hands on the chair across from her. "I'm sorry if I startled you, but I thought you knew I was still here."

Gena stood up abruptly, making the robe swirl about her feet. She felt ill-at-ease. For one thing, she hadn't a touch of makeup on. Oh, what did it matter, anyway?

"Would you care for something to eat?"

"Please. The same as you had, if it wouldn't be too much trouble."

She kept her back to him while she cooked, and he sank wearily into a chair.

"Do you know what that braid signifies in this country . . . ?" From his tone, he seemed determined to goad her.

"Spare me."

"It means," he began, ignoring her barbed tone, "that you are a maiden."

"Then I shall braid it every day!"

While he ate, she washed her dishes, finishing up by wiping off the electric stovetop. That chore finished, she turned away from the range, only to catch one of her long blue sleeves on a hot burner, jerking her wrist backward onto the circular coil, searing her tender skin.

Alex was beside her almost at once, lifting her arm free and pushing her none too gently over to the sink to run cold water over the burned area. The gushing spray immediately eased the pain. Gena leaned forward over the sink, her knees wobbly. Alex towered over her, grasping her waist with one arm while the other hand insured that her wrist remained under the stream of icy liquid.

"You need a keeper," he grumbled.

Gena stirred at his words, but her irritated movement only brought her that much closer to him. Then, incredibly, she felt the hand at her waist move a few inches past her curving waistline to her hip.

He stepped away from her, his face dark with anger.

"What are you trying to prove? Go and put some clothes on!"

Her voice turned as frigid as the water splashing over her wrist. "Are you blind? I'm covered from my neck down."

"And what about underneath?" he growled. "I won't have you running around half-naked. If one of my men should come in . . ."

Gena turned the tap off, then faced him. Uncaring that water was dripping down her gown, she quite deliberately unzipped the robe, shrugging it off her creamy shoulders. The demure white nightgown she wore underneath was displayed.

"Now do you believe me?"

Alex didn't answer at once. His dark eyes were drawn to the flesh visible through the fine cotton. Her quick movement had thrust her chest out, outlining her generous breasts. They strained at the delicate material.

When his hands reached for her, she fully expected him to give her a shake. Instead, he grasped the edges of her open robe and pulled them together. He rezipped it.

Gena jerked away from him. He was actually smiling! She felt confused, then angry.

"What, may I ask, is so funny?" she demanded.

"I might tell you one day," he promised lightly.

She was suddenly conscious of how much her burn was bothering her again. She ran more water over it to ease the pain.

"Is it worse?" he inquired politely, stuffing his hands into the back pockets of his jeans.

"No. It feels just great!"

"I can see that you're determined to make our living together a trial," he sighed. "Look, if your wrist needs a light covering I can let you have some gauze bandages that will at least keep it from rubbing on things until you see a doctor in the morning."

"I'm not going to a doctor for this little burn."

"Have it your way. Well, I'd better go and change," he announced, watching her pat her injured wrist dry.

"When will you be back?"

"Why?" His tone was suddenly suspicious.

With a snooty toss of her head, she said, "So that I can have Kostas safely out of here by then, of course!" The minute she had said it, she was sorry. Why did she keep trying to upset Alex? And why did she keep choosing Kostas as her weapon? She tried to ward him off with her good arm. "Alex, I didn't mean it. . . ."

He picked her up almost effortlessly, slinging her over his shoulder. They left the confines of the kitchen that way, despite her shrieking demands that he put her down.

In less than half a minute she was tossed onto the sofa in the main salon. Not knowing what he planned on doing to her, she flipped over on her stomach, maintaining a hold on a silky brown throw pillow. She squeezed her eyes shut and waited. Her entire body tensed and she clung that much tighter to the plump cushion, burying her chin in its elegant fabric. And waited.

His grim laughter reached her. "Perfect."

With the first sharp crack as his flat palm hit her derriere, Gena yelped in disbelief. Her struggles to turn around were thwarted by a firm, steady pressure applied to her back. Six more spankings were administered before he lifted his knee off the point by which he held her captive.

"How . . . could you?" she choked out, rubbing a hand over the smarting area.

"You asked for it!"

"Well, you didn't have to beat me!" she fumed, rolling over to face him. He was studying one of his paintings.

He ignored her complaints. "You appeared to like this room earlier. Mother told the decorators what color scheme to use. I find it peaceful. . . ."

"I thought Sofia had helped you," she said angrily, grimly blowing on her reddened wrist, which was hurting again. The singed cuff of her robe had just scraped it, making her curse. She looked up guiltily, but Alex was gone.

It took her a full minute of pacing back and forth in the upstairs hallway before she could summon up enough courage to knock on his door.

"Come in."

Gena stared at the white door open-mouthed, taken aback by his casually stated invitation. "All . . . I want are the bandages you said I could have," she called loudly.

"And I repeat—come in," he said in an impatient tone. "Don't worry, I'm fully clothed."

She pushed the door open.

"I'm sorry to bother you. . . ." Her chin dropped and she remained riveted by the door, watching as he casually unzipped his tailored black pants so that he could tuck in his shirttails.

"Help yourself. Look in the mirrored cabinet in my bathroom. In there." He jerked his head, motioning to a point behind him.

Gena moved hastily in the direction he had indicated. She refused to look to either side, trying to ignore the unmade bed that seemed to dominate the large room with its four-postered magnificence.

She was still searching through the many shelves when he came up behind her. "Having trouble?"

She nodded. "And when I move my wrist, it hurts."

A large, tanned hand reached over her, immediately securing a small box of sterile gauze wrapping. "Turn your wrist over."

She shook her head stubbornly.

"Gena . . ." His voice held weary anger. "Do I have to repeat that spanking?"

She grabbed the box. "Over my dead body!"

Just as his hand snaked out to seize her, the phone in his bedroom rang.

"Let it ring," he said harshly.

"But . . ."

"I said let it ring!"

"It *could* be the hospital, Alex. I know you think it's Kostas, but . . ." She started as a hand clamped down over her shoulder. When the last ring had died he let her go, almost pushing her toward the door.

"I know the way out," she said coldly. But as she stepped onto the rich gray carpet that covered the floor of his bedroom, she stumbled, tripping on the edge of her robe. She was caught from behind just before her knees would have touched the thick rug. She felt hard fingers dig into the soft flesh under her breasts, then his arms gathered her up so that she stood straight, her feet under her once more.

She swayed, brushing a hand over her forehead. "I suppose I should thank you." She smiled weakly, intentionally ignoring his stern expression.

He let her move away. "What's wrong with you? You act like a nervous child." His dark eyes appraised her, watching her while she fingered the singed cuff of the robe's right sleeve. "What do you think I'm going to do to you?"

Her cheeks flushed and he swore softly. "Did I hurt you?" he asked then, noting that one hand was pressed to her ribs.

"What are a few more bruises?"

His chiselled features hardened once more. "It seems you are bent on arousing my anger, but I refuse to take the bait. I am not some young boy who can be easily manipulated. I am a man. Remember that. You, on the other hand, are trying your wings, using your womanly charms, testing reactions. You are enticing, provoking, sometimes unknowingly sensual. . . ." He followed her back into his bedroom.

"I don't know what you're talking about!" Her goal was the door that led to the hall. In her haste, the skirt of her gown swirled around her legs, outlining the swaying motion of her hips.

"Look in the mirror then." He sank onto the edge of his bed and bent to pick up a shoe. "And stay clear of Kostas."

She turned to look at him after she had stepped

113

out of his room. He was slipping into a suit jacket that exactly matched the pants he wore.

"He might not be as . . . considerate as I was."

Before she could think of a reply the phone shrilled again. "It's for you. . . ."

He was holding the receiver out for her, extending it so that she had to retrace her steps and stand next to him. "Sweet girl!" were the first words that were uttered against her ear.

"Kostas . . . please!" she pleaded weakly, glancing up at Alex.

"What time shall I come for you this evening? In an hour, say?" he persisted.

"I can't. Not tonight. Grandmother has her operation tomorrow and . . ."

"And it will do you good to come out with me. It will lessen your worries for a while, hmm? I will be by for you in one hour, then."

Click. He had hung up.

"Are you going out with him? After everything I told you?" he fairly shouted.

Gena wanted to cover her ears and cower. His brows were drawn together in a forbidding dark line over black eyes that were as hard as flint. Her mouth worked tremulously, but not a word came out.

"Well?" he glowered, shifting his weight to the other foot.

She fluttered a hand helplessly. "I . . . Yes!"

"*Christos!*" He rubbed his chin as if in pain. "What do I have to do to convince you?"

"I'm sure he's only taking me out to dinner. There's no harm in *that!*"

"We Greeks eat late. What is he planning between six and nine o'clock?"

"Ask him."

"I will not be here. I am late in getting to the hospital as it is." He paused. "If he so much as lays a hand on you . . . If he even tries kissing you . . . I want to know. You understand?" he seethed, reaching out to wrap a large hand around her braid to draw her closer.

Gena's heart gave a fearful lurch. "You . . . you're hurting me."

His piercing look roved over her face and for a moment his grip on her hair actually tightened, making her cry out. "Believe me, Gena, this is nothing to what you will endure if you are not back and safely in your bed before I get in."

The long braid swung free. "What time . . . ?"

"Am I coming back this evening?" He lifted a shoulder. "It all depends. After I assure myself that Mother is settled in for the night I have to see someone. . . ."

A knife seemed to slice through her heart. That "someone" was Sofia, of course. Gena looked down at her slippered feet, envisioning their reunion—she came out of her reverie with an abrupt jerk.

In her mind, she had substituted her own uninhibited form for Sofia's faceless one. It was her own body that she saw, moving in response to Alex's hard, ready frame. Gena pressed a hand to her heaving breasts. As from a distance, she heard Alex speak.

"We can talk tomorrow. Maybe . . . things will be different then. You're tired."

They walked to the door together. "Leave a note for Kostas, saying you are staying in, that you need your sleep," he urged, touching her shoulder.

"No, I'll go."

His voice grew taut. "Have it your way then." And without another word he headed for the stairs.

When Kostas arrived, she was dressed and waiting. As she opened the door he bowed, but not before his dark eyes openly admired her.

"You look enchanting."

She felt slightly uneasy when his eyes wandered over her bare shoulders as she picked up her triangular silk shawl.

"You shouldn't say such things to me. We barely know each other."

"But you blush so becomingly, Gena. And since when is it wrong for a man to tell a woman how lovely she is? Or to kiss her so . . . ?" He leaned sideways as if to place his mouth against her bare neck.

Gena avoided his advances by moving back a step. "If you don't behave, I won't go anywhere with you!" she sputtered. For the first time she realized just how very much alone they were.

He smiled, as if sensing her nervousness. "Do you know that I find you utterly refreshing? Any

other woman would not be so . . . ah . . . re-
served, shall we say?" He looked around. "And
where is your uncle?"

"He left for the hospital shortly after you called."

She noticed that Kostas seemed pleased. Perhaps he thought that Alex considered him trustwor-
thy. That was almost funny.

Kostas touched her lightly, stroking a finger down
her bare forearm. "Let us go then. I want to show
you around Athens. Then we shall have supper,
dance maybe . . . It is all part of my grand plan."

She looked at him suspiciously as they waited for
the elevator.

"On my honor," he said, raising both hands, "I
promise to be the perfect gentleman. The only
thing I shall insist on is bestowing a chaste good
night kiss on those utterly delectable lips of
yours. . . ." But his eyes burned brightly as he
spoke.

A short while later, they were seated in the back
of the small, gray limousine that had been parked in
front of Alex's building. "My driver is going to take
us on a little tour, though, of course, it is much
better to explore Athens on foot. The traffic tends
to be frantic at times." He smiled knowledgeably.

"I know," she agreed. "I had a wild ride from the
airport to the Hilton. Now I know why the taxi
driver had a saint's medallion *plus* his worry beads
hanging from the rearview mirror!"

Kostas frowned. "You were forced to take a
taxi?"

"There was a bit of a mix-up." Gena could have

kicked herself for being so open with him. She didn't want to get Nick in trouble.

"Didn't Alexander know you were coming?" he persisted.

To deny his awareness would have been an outright lie, so Gena merely nodded.

"Then why weren't you met?"

Gena could sense his growing anger and she tried to reassure him. "Everything turned out fine, so why does it matter? Let's not ruin the evening," she soothed.

His moustache still bristled, but he appeared to relax. He patted the hand that covered her small black dress bag.

"We will soon be coming into the city. My driver has taken a route that will give you a good view of the Acropolis."

For the next hour he concentrated on answering all her questions and pointing out spots of interest, adding a great deal of past history as well.

Halfway along Venizelos Avenue, as they approached Omnia Square, he pointed toward a collection of marble buildings.

"The academy, the university and the library," he announced, "and despite their impression of antiquity, they were built in the nineteenth century."

As they reached Omnia Square Kostas pressed a button, lowering the window between them and their chauffeur. The car slowed after he issued orders to the driver.

"Now here we come to what some people refer to as Athens' Piccadilly." He grinned. "It is a vibrant, exciting place, no? There are theaters, fountains, flower-sellers, junk shops, coffee shops . . . everything."

Gena nodded, entranced. At last, a look at the personal side of the crowded city.

"Some cafes remain open until midnight, but the shops close soon; it's nearing eight o'clock." He gestured with a sweeping motion. "This is one of the twin hearts of Athens; the other is Syntagma, or as it is also called, Constitution Square. We traveled past it a while ago."

"It's very kind of you to take me around like this."

"It's my pleasure." He quirked an eyebrow in her direction. "I hope you're hungry. We're on our way to an early dinner—by my standards, at least."

"I'm pleased that we're eating this soon. I must get back at a decent hour. With Grandmother in the hospital, I feel very guilty being out at all. Besides, Alex would be angry if I stayed out late," she finished with a smile, to soften her last words.

Kostas' own smile was cynical. "Do not worry about Papa Bear. He is with Sofia by now. If he returns at all, I would be most surprised!"

Her smile froze.

He went on, waving a hand to dismiss their discussion of Alex. "After we dine, I want to show you my yacht at the marina in Vouliagmeni. It is on the coastline, not far from Athens. You will like it.

119

Later this week I would like to spend the day there with you. We could go swimming and lunch on board my vessel."

Gena barely heard him. The crowded buildings and streets passed in a blur before her misty eyes. The thought of Alex with Sofia . . . all the night through . . . was unendurable.

"This isn't your car, Kostas," she objected as he led her to a low-slung white Porsche. But when he dangled the keys in front of her face she felt foolish. She was glad it was getting dark. Her face turned hot. Dinner had been delicious, and perhaps she had had too much wine.

He chuckled as they drove away from the night-spot. "I should have told you I would be driving. Will you forgive me?"

Gena looked with interest at the neon-lit clubs that were coming into view. "I might. Where are we going?"

"To my yacht, via a less-traveled route."

"Isn't it getting late? Really, Kostas, I . . ."

"Late? What is late? Are you going to turn into a pumpkin if I don't get you back by midnight, I wonder?" A serious note crept into his voice. "Have you thought again about what I asked this morning? I am serious about this. Most serious, Gena," he repeated, keeping his eyes on the road ahead. "I know my feelings for you are not to either of your uncle's likings. Alex's especially. Ever since Helene . . . but that is another story."

Gena's throat tightened at his revealing words. So Alex had been right after all.

It was at this point that she took a good look at the rutted, unpaved road that lay ahead. The main highway had been filled with bright, fast-paced traffic, but theirs was the only car on this side road. It was easy to see why.

Suddenly she was frightened. What did she actually know about this man? Next to nothing, a little voice answered her. Just that he was rich, unmarried . . . and at times ruthless. He wasn't even a trusted friend of Alex's. What trusted friend would take a friend's wife to bed? And he had practically admitted to her that he had been involved with Helene, hadn't he? What if he wasn't planning to bring her back to Athens at all?

At least she had her wits about her again; the air had helped to clear her head of the wine. Her partly opened window drew the cooler night air in, caressing her hair and face, awakening her to reality.

Kostas' sudden movement jerked her out of her private thoughts. He swore softly and braked, bringing the car to a complete stop at the side of the road, the wayside brush almost touching her side of the car.

"The car is behaving strangely. I am going to check the tires." He gave her a reassuring smile, then ducked so as not to bump his head before sliding out of his seat. "Stay in the car."

Her heart pounding, Gena didn't know whether to believe him or not. Just then he came round, leaning his forearms on the fully lowered window frame, looking across at her.

"They look fine. It must be the state of the road."

Gena forced herself to smile in response.

Moonlight glistened on the hood of the white car and its reflective beams lit a portion of the lush leather interior as well. Gena was unaware that its probing rays dusted her throat and bare shoulders, or that its dull glow dipped low to outline her braless bodice, detailing the fully rounded breasts that lay under the black fabric.

When Kostas finally settled back down in his seat, minus the pale gray suitcoat which he tossed behind him, Gena missed the look he threw her.

"You are a beautiful young woman."

Her stomach fluttered nervously.

"I noticed that you have a mark on your wrist," he began conversationally. He leaned his head on the window he had just closed, and partly faced her.

Gena nodded. "It was an accident." The words almost stuck in her throat. What now?

"How did it happen?" he asked softly. A hand reached out to touch the hurt spot.

She was just about to open her mouth and explain further, when she felt his hand drop to her knee and brush aside the ruffles at the hem of her skirt.

"No!" she cried, using all her strength to push him away. She shuddered, repelled by the intimate caress.

"Stop behaving like a child," he said mildly, not at all put off by her alarm. "You knew when you came out with me that I would make love to you."

Gena stared at him open-mouthed. This couldn't be happening. Her feelings were so mixed, she didn't know whether to laugh or cry. Was he serious?

"I intend to marry you—if I find out that I am your first lover." He fingered his moustache speculatively. "And I think I will be. You have that look. . . ." He chuckled. "Do not look so fearful. This car was not built to accomodate a seduction. I shall be content to wait until we reach my yacht." His voice lowered to a sensual pitch. "Come now, Gena. Give me a preview. Show me what will be mine." His fingers tugged playfully at the elastic neckline of her dress.

She pushed his hand away. Her adrenaline was flowing; fury welled up in her, replacing her nervousness. "Keep your hands off me!" Her eyes blazed purple sparks. "If I wanted you to make love to me, do you think I'd be sitting half out the door? I have no intention of marrying you, Kostas. Not next week, next month, or next year. Have you got that? You just try making another pass at me and I'll scratch your eyes out!"

He had the audacity to laugh. "My dear little spitfire!" But he made no move to drive on.

"Are you going to take me back to Kifissia, or am I going to walk?"

"This is getting tiresome. I told you before . . ."

She interrupted him. "Have you thought what Alex is going to do about all this . . . ?"

"Alex can go to Hades for all I care!" he answered. A mocking smile twisted his mouth.

If she was shocked by his attitude she tried not to show it.

"Alex and I have not been true friends for a long time. You don't look perplexed by my admission, I see." He stared at her for a long moment. "He must have told you then. . . . Well, now you can hear my version of the story. His wife had left him; she simply walked out, then arrived on my doorstep begging to stay for a few days until her new lover came for her—the man she had left Alex for. Contrary to what Alex believes, I never touched her. At that time, such a thing would have been against my code of honor." He lifted a shoulder. "She stayed two—three days. A month later she was dead. I know he still blames me. Maybe he loved her after all." He drew a breath. "But now, because of that fermented mistrust, it will give me the greatest pleasure to punish him through you, his niece. It will give me the utmost satisfaction to see him reel with shock when I tell him that I have slept with you!"

"You're mad! Do you honestly believe I'll let you do what you want with me?" She swung her purse at him, aiming for his face. Before he had a chance to change gears, she scrambled from the car.

A scraggly, half-dead bush clawed at her arms and legs before she could duck. Then she began to run back to the turn-off by the highway. She heard the car's engine purr as it turned and came up to the right of her. But she kept running.

Fear made her increase her pace. Thank heavens she jogged in Central Park from time to time, or she would never even have thought she stood a chance. She winced again, turning her ankle. Her dress sandals weren't made for this torture. Without a second thought, she slowed and kicked them off, leaving them where they fell. Her chest was beginning to hurt. She panted, gasping for breath, trying to keep to the side of the road where there was an occasional patch of grass for her aching feet. Her heart was pounding madly. Her greatest fear was that Kostas might decide to chase after her on foot. At least he couldn't do her any harm while he continued to drive. . . .

He was keeping pace with her, waiting . . . She could just see the white Porsche from the corner of her eye. She heard herself moan. If she could only stop . . . just for a minute to get her breath back, she thought, drawing an agonizing gasp . . .

"Enjoying yourself?" he called.

Hot tears gathered in the corners of her eyes, making them smart. She musn't cry, she told herself desperately. She could barely see where she was going as it was. Hair pins fell from the casual swirl on top of her head, sending the dark, thick mass tumbling past her shoulders, but she was oblivious to everything except breathing and running. She pressed a hand to her racing heart. How she yearned to stop.

An idea hit her. What if she *did* stop? He would

too, and . . . Her plan was so simple, it just might work. It was worth a try. She couldn't last much longer.

Gena issued a silent prayer, then slowed and came to a halt on quivering legs. While she drew in several gulping breaths, Kostas continued to drive a little ahead as if he didn't quite believe she was through running. He eventually stepped from his car, leaving it idling. Gena walked toward him, her head hanging docilely. One quick look told her all she needed. His stance was casual, his expression intolerably smug as he rested an elbow on the top of the door.

It was now or never.

With all her remaining strength, Gena sprinted forward and pushed at Kostas, sending him sprawling back into a clump of young evergreens that banked a shallow incline. Before he could scramble to his feet, she was in the driver's seat, shifting the Porsche's powerful transmission. Her breath was coming in tortured whimpers. For a few sickening moments she didn't think the car was going to react when she floored its accelerator, but just as she reached for the leather-padded door to slam it shut, the Porsche leaped ahead, kicking up a mound of sand and pebbles with its rear tires.

There was never a more welcome sight than the bright lights of Athens. It seemed to take forever to reach Kifissia, and when she pulled into the apartment house's parking area she dropped her weary head onto the steering wheel, exhausted. She made her way slowly toward the front door of the building on tender, sore feet. Lucky for her the guards were out of sight, though she did hear voices. While the elevator whisked her to the top floor, she made a hopeless attempt at tidying herself, but soon gave up. A weary shoulder lifted and shrugged. At least she didn't have to worry about being greeted by Alex, she thought dully, her mouth twisting. He would undoubtedly be with Sofia.

The key Alex had given her fit into the lock smoothly, and she felt her way into the dark entranceway, groping for a light switch, then thought better of it and shut the door with the weight of her exhausted body, letting herself slip to the parquet floor where she sat as if dazed.

A tear slid down her cheek, then another. She sniffled noisily, wiping them away with the backs of her hands, then blinked her eyes, trying to accustom them to the dark. The apartment wasn't completely devoid of light as she had at first thought. A faint light had been left on upstairs. She must have forgotten to turn it off after her.

She wiggled her toes experimentally. There was nothing left of the bottoms of her pantyhose. A few flyaway and very dirty shreds decorated her ankles. On impulse she lifted first one leg, then the other, and pushed them off, whimpering aloud as the sheer material snagged on her painfully scratched legs.

"Now comes the hard part," she murmured, grabbing for the purse she had somehow hung onto throughout her ordeal. She eyed the stairway as if it were her enemy and struggled to her feet.

It was then that she noticed the dark, still figure sitting on the bottom step watching her every movement.

Gena gave a little scream and fell, her limp form curled into a tired heap in front of the door.

The man who had waited for her return rose and made his way toward her. His eyes were as black as the clothes he wore.

6

꘎ꞏꞏꞏꞏꞏꞏꞏ꘎

She came to just as he lowered her onto his bed.

"It was *you!*" Her chin trembled and she had a difficult time keeping back the tears. "For a moment I thought . . ." She put a hand over her eyes to hide the pain that was as much emotional as physical. "It isn't like you think, Alex."

"*You dare to lie to me?*"

The hostility in his voice cut her like a knife. She could feel his hands on either side of her as he leaned over her still, tense form, the bed giving slightly as he balanced part of his weight on the rumpled bedspread.

"I'll kill him!" He lifted a hand and ran a finger down a scratch on her pale arm, tracing its redness. "There is a rip here," he pointed out in an incensed tone, pressing warm fingers to a seam under an arm, "and another here." Again he touched her dress, his hand coming to rest near her hip. "Your hair is in disarray, you are covered with scratches, shoeless, dirty . . . Whatever he did to you—was it worth it?"

The seconds ticked by.

"Let me up." There was a dreary, hollow feeling in her chest. She felt the bed spring up as he moved away from her. Gena rose, trying not to act as weak as she felt.

"Where do you think you're going?" In an instant he had pushed her flat again.

She avoided looking directly into his face, her head turned to one side. "To my room," she answered dully. He would never believe that Kostas hadn't used her. Perhaps even used her willingly. Never in a million years, she reflected.

"You need medical attention and someone to help you with your bath. And since we don't have a maid or a nurse handy, I am going to substitute for both."

Gena shrank back. "No!"

"If I have to rip those clothes off you, I will," he stated fiercely. "Now are you going to undress, or shall I do it for you? For heaven's sake, stop being coy. If you can run off into the bushes with a man you've known only a few hours, why should you mind if I see you?"

Gena nearly gagged. She turned away from him, willing herself not to be sick. She must have fainted, because when she opened her eyes it was to feel

Alex pulling her arms out of the sleeves of her dress. Water was running somewhere. Suddenly she was fighting like a wildcat, clawing, kicking . . . Her hands connected with the side of his face, leaving a white mark where she struck. Then she was pinned to the bed, unable to move. Their faces were so close that Gena was able to see a faint mask of perspiration build on his forehead and upper lip.

"Why didn't you fight like this with him?" he shouted hoarsely.

"Alex . . . Alex. Hold me. Just hold me. I was so scared." Her voice wavered on a high-pitched note. "I ran. Ran from him." She paused, her teeth chattering from nervous tension. "When I stopped, he . . . got out of his car, and . . ."

He closed his eyes, and his head bent, their foreheads touching. Gena felt his ragged breath mingling with her own.

"Tell me," he groaned. "I must know what he did to you."

Her mouth moved closer to his as she explained, "Nothing. He did nothing, Alex. I . . . I managed to push him in . . . into a ditch, then I took off in his Porsche. . . ." Her misty glance met his level one. "If you don't believe me," she gulped, "go . . . look in your parking lot."

His hands moved away from her captured ones, cradling her face instead, and his hard form impressed itself onto hers, spreading a fire throughout her own body that at once excited and shocked her. There was an intense throbbing deep inside her that cried out for fulfillment. She whispered his name and her tired arms moved to encircle him.

"No!" In one fluid motion he was off the bed, turning his back to her, his breath coming in short, quick rasps. He motioned for her to follow him into his bathroom.

She came to stand next to him just as he turned the water off. The marble tub was nearly full.

"Get undressed." A muscle worked in his cheek.

What did it matter, she thought dully, placing her watch on a nearby shelf. She couldn't possibly embarrass herself any more than she already had. What had made her behave that way? She had practically asked him to make love to her. As if he had any more love to give . . . after visiting his mistress.

She tugged at her sleeves, pulling her arms out, intending to slide the dress past her hips to the floor, but it was difficult to accomplish with him watching. All she could think about was how he had tried to undress her while she lay on the bed, and her fingers grew stiff, stumbling over their task.

With hands that were surprisingly gentle, he took over, until at last she was standing in only her lacy, black bikini panties.

"Get in the bathtub."

"With . . . with these on?" she asked wonderingly, her arms folded protectingly across her breasts.

His teeth snapped together. "Suit yourself."

"Turn around."

"What do you think I am—a monk? I know what the female body looks like, Gena. It holds no surprises for me," he ended, almost shouting.

Her scratches smarted as she settled her naked form into the warm water. She sat stiffly, flushing under his gaze.

"Do you mind if I wash in private?"

"I'm staying. And if you don't get on with it, I'll do the soaping myself!"

When she was nearly done, he said, "You're half asleep. Give me the facecloth and I'll wash your back and legs."

She relinquished her hold on the soapy square of material and turned so that he could start on her shoulders.

Gena yawned. "If anyone had told me last week that I would be letting you bathe me, I would have told them they were mad!" Her eyes were almost closing. "It's funny that I can't even imagine Kostas . . ."

He jerked her chin into profile. "Be careful, Gena."

"Hmm?" Her lids drooped.

"Is this some kind of game with you?" he demanded.

"What . . . do you mean?"

"If I didn't know that you were so worn out, I would swear that you were being deliberately tantalizing."

"You hate me." She sniffed. "And you always will. . . ."

"How I wish!" he replied, soaping the cloth. "Rest your legs over the edge."

"You seem to know what you're doing. . . ." A question hung in the air.

"Oh, sure. Every time I take a woman out, I lure her to my bathroom, then I bathe her," he said sarcastically. "Can't you just see the headlines if this story gets out? 'Greek shipping magnate Andreas admits that his fetish is . . .'"

Gena gurgled. "You don't do this for a living, then?" Her head was thrown back as she laughed weakly, unknowingly exposing her wet, glistening breasts for his inspection, their dark tips puckered in the chill.

He stood, his manner turning suddenly cool and businesslike. "Wash your hair. I'm going to find a robe for you."

She had just tucked a large blue bath towel around her dripping body when he reappeared, a short white towelling robe over one arm. She began to rub her hair, trying to get it dry enough to comb.

"This will take forever to dry," she sighed. "Even with my blow dryer."

"I can do it for you," he said calmly, searching his cabinet for a tube of medicated ointment. When he found it he proceeded to dab some on one of his fingers, then gently applied it to her worst scrapes. "There. Now into your bed so that I can check the cuts on your feet."

She swayed on her feet, barely able to keep her eyes open. "Alex, I . . . I'm so tired. . . ."

The next thing she knew she was being put gently back on his bed.

"Your comb?"

"In my purse—over there on the floor."

He unwound the towel from her hair, then began. Sometime later she felt warm air hit her face from time to time. And then she slept.

She awoke, her body tossing about anxiously. "Alex?" she called. A form stirred in a chair not far from the bed.

"What is it?" he asked tensely.

"Whose room is this?"

"Mine."

"Why don't you sleep in my bed, then?" she whispered. "You can't sit up all night."

Silence.

"Well?" she prodded.

"Gena, shut up and go back to sleep."

"I was only trying to help!"

She heard him sigh.

"What time is it?"

"Three o'clock."

"Have you slept at all?"

"Gena!"

She kicked at her covers.

"Don't do that."

"How can you see what I'm doing? It's pitch dark in here." She sat up. "I'm going to my own bed. . . . Oh!" She hadn't a stitch on. No robe, no towel. She was very quiet for a minute.

"Alex . . . ?"

"What is it *now?*"

135

"I don't think I can get back to sleep."

"Gena, I've had a very trying day. . . ." he began.

"I can't sleep with you sitting up all night." she interrupted him. Inexplicably, she was very near to tears.

"What would you have me do—sleep with you?"

She shrugged in the darkness. "I can't imagine you'd be interested. After all, we both understand how it is between you and Sofia."

"You little witch. Are you insinuating that I was in her bed tonight?" he hissed.

Gena made out his approaching form just before he sat down next to her on the bed.

"I assumed you were dying to get back to Athens for that reason."

"I wanted to get away from you!" He heard her sharp gasp of pain. "Damn you. . . ."

Gena hurtled to the other side of the bed, her chest tight with repressed sobs. He caught her by the hair, dragging her back, forcing her to lie full length across the bed.

"Let me go!" Gena cried, trying to push aside the hand that was spread across her stomach.

"Never." His lips were by her ear, tasting her, making her lose her breath. Then he was touching her, making her respond until she moaned aloud with pleasure, her little gasps and noises echoing until they blended into one long shuddering galaxy of sighs as a mounting feeling of arousal overwhelmed her, then quieted her again. He lifted his lips from her breasts, smiling.

"Alex . . ." Her eyes closed.

"Sleep." He bent and kissed her parted lips.

"Don't go," she sighed, snuggling close to his chest.

"I won't." Her deep, even breathing was his only answer.

The first streaks of light awakened her. She was lying on her left side, facing the cream wall, watching a shaft of brightness dance its path over her hip, outlining Alex's hand lying warm and heavy on it.

When she first opened her eyes, the feel of his body at her back had startled her, then she remembered and her face flushed at the memory. How was she to face him today?

Her toes curled. The hand on her hip was lazily traveling upward over the silky sheet. His breath was warm on her bare shoulder.

"Are you awake now?" he teased lightly.

She nodded, not trusting herself to speak.

"How are you feeling?"

"I . . . I'm not sure."

He laughed quietly. "You're shy and embarrassed. Admit it." He nipped her earlobe. "Turn around. I won't hurt you."

"You didn't hurt me last night. . . ." she said in a little rush, half-breathless from his nearness. "How could you have . . . I mean, you didn't . . ."

He turned her so that she lay on her back.

137

"Are you disappointed that I didn't?" His finger brushed across her lips and trailed down her throat. She didn't object when it settled further down, her breast swelling under his gentle, arousing massage.

"Tell me that you are mine to have, Gena. I want to hear you say it." His voice was quiet, though there was a strain in it. "We both know where this will lead . . . if I keep touching you. . . . If you don't want us to become lovers, say it now!" He cleared his throat. "A courier brought your adoption papers last night. . . . I no longer have to torment myself that you are my sister's child. . . . Well?"

She couldn't think clearly, yet he appeared to be so calm. How *could* she think? He had pulled away the sheet, exposing her nakedness to his eyes. If only he loved her as she knew she loved him! Everything would be so easy then.

"It . . . won't last," she croaked. Then she gasped as she felt his tongue caress the delicate hollows of her throat.

He raised his head. "Because of the difference in our ages?"

Her head moved from left to right. "Everybody will know. . . ." she said weakly.

"Eventually, yes. But for the time being we can keep it quiet. For Mother's sake." He waited a moment, then asked, "Your answer is yes, Gena?"

She glanced down at his tanned, muscled frame. A black pair of snug-fitting underwear hugged his lean hips. "You could have anyone you wanted. . . ."

"I want *you*."

His arrogant tone frightened her, but she was determined to pursue her train of thought. "You might for a while, but then what? Will you tire of me, too?" Her tone thickened. "But then I forgot this is only a summer dalliance for you. . . . I shall be returning to New York. You can go back to your mistress. . . . I . . ."

She stopped speaking. A punishing kiss assaulted her parted lips, then another, leaving her gasping for air as he finally raised his head. A tear squeezed from beneath her closed lids. "Do you want another spanking?" he asked roughly.

"No." Her voice was a whimper.

"Then don't talk so foolishly!"

"I can't help it," she sniffled, "I've never done . . . this . . . before!"

"I hope not!" he exploded, his eyes assessing her grimly. "If I'm not the first, tell me now, because when I take you . . ."

"Oh, Alex!" She offered her lips.

His hand cupped her breast. Heart pounding, she raised herself up on one elbow and kissed him on the lips, daring to pull him with her as she lay back down.

"You want me." It was a statement.

Gena looked away, then nodded. There was no turning back now. She waited expectantly, her body tense with longing and fear.

The bed moved, and suddenly he was standing beside it. "I could be very selfish right now and take what you offer," he said softly, "but instead, I shall force us both to wait a few days." He threw the covers over her in one swift movement. "And believe me, it will be sheer torture!" A humorous glint appeared in his dark eyes. "Can you wait that long, my beauty?"

His actions stunned her, and she stared at him open-mouthed. What did he mean? When she didn't answer him, he laid a hand on her flushed cheek, asking, "Are you feeling all right?"

She glared at him.

"I was only going to ask you to make us some breakfast." He sighed and straightened. "We have to be at the hospital by eight."

"Alex, you're not making sense. People—normal people that is—don't turn their emotions off and on like a . . . a faucet! First you make mad, passionate love to me, now you talk about waiting. . . ." She looked at him helplessly.

"Correct." He padded calmly toward the bathroom.

Enraged by his refusal to explain, Gena leaped out of bed and shrugged on the robe he had found for her the night before, following him into the smaller confines of his bathroom. A pair of strong hands turned her around and marched her back into the bedroom.

"Darling, I need some privacy. Whatever is bothering you can wait a few minutes. Perhaps after we're married I won't mind the distraction, but until then . . ."

Her anger dissolved. Married. Her brain echoed with the word. She backed away from the door. He couldn't have meant it. She had to get out of his room before she imagined anything else. . . .

The smell of coffee greeted her when she stepped out of her room, carrying her shoes.

"Sore feet?" he asked sympathetically, at the same time handing her a cup of the steaming brew. Then he chuckled. "Nick phoned. I suppose you heard the ring?" He paused to hand her a container of cream. "Kostas is in the hospital, too."

Her eyes flew to his face.

"His ankle is broken. That mighty push of yours gave him something he'll remember for a while! Of course, Nick knows nothing of how it happened. I'll have to stop by his room and give him my regards."

"He told me he never touched Helene, Alex, and I believe him, strangely enough." When silence greeted her statement, she asked him quietly, "Would you like some breakfast?"

The thin cigar he had just lit was stabbed out with a savage twist. "No," he refused sharply. "And I will thank you not to discuss my private views and my life with anyone else in the future." The pale blue of his shirt gleamed crisply against his tanned throat. "If there is anything you must learn, it is that. I value my privacy. The less I am in the public eye, the better," he ground out. "And, as my wife, you will learn to be just as circumspect."

"I . . . I've been meaning to talk to you about that," she interjected.

"There's nothing to discuss, Gena. We're getting

married in two days," he said in a voice that had a final ring to it.

"But . . ." She got no further.

"I need a wife. My daughter needs a mother, someone she has a rapport with, and," his eyes raked her as he spoke, "you definitely need a husband—you proved that much upstairs!"

Gone was the tender man who had slept beside her. In his place was the old Alex—cruel and demanding. How could she have believed one person could change that much? She felt numbed by his cold, calculating attitude.

"I am *not* volunteering for the job. Ask Sofia." She felt the tears rise in her throat as she spoke. Then a sudden thought occured to her. "Or doesn't your mistress care for children?"

"Does it matter?" he asked in a bored voice.

Gena forced herself to take a drink from her coffee cup.

"Why don't you just hire someone to take care of Ana? Or better yet, ship her off to a boarding school. I'm sure that would be satisfactory to Sofia." She jumped to her feet, her eyes flashing with suspicious brightness. "*I* wouldn't marry you under pain of death!" She fled the table, tears splashing onto her crisp white knit top.

The exhausting day was over. Grandmother's operation was safely over, but she and Alex . . . well, the less said about that the better. Gena craned her head and reached to lift her wristwatch from the bedside table. It read exactly midnight, just as she thought it would. After all, she had checked it five minutes before, hadn't she? She stared at the pale ceiling for a while, then reached over to turn off the bedside lamp. She curled over on her side, tucking a hand under the pillow.

What was it Nick had said when he dropped her off? Don't wait up for Alex . . . ? As if she would. He had been at the hospital, but had gone off on his own rather than stay with Gena and Nick. Even when he had put in a brief appearance to report the success of the operation he had not smiled, or even bothered to bestow more than a cursory glance on her. She hadn't seen him since.

Gena punched her pillow. Well, if that's the way he wants it . . . fine! Yet . . .

"Stop tormenting yourself. It's for the best," she whispered into the empty room. "Just imagine being married to him!" It would be heaven . . . or hell. Maybe a little of both.

It was on those thoughts that she fell asleep.

All too soon it was morning again. She murmured protestingly when the alarm went off, and turned over. Then she blinked. What alarm? She propped herself up on an elbow, rubbing the sleep from her eyes and reached for her watch, only to discover Alex's sleeping form between herself and her goal.

"The next time the phone rings, reach over and answer it, will you?" he muttered groggily.

"Get out of here!" she choked out, overcome with rage. "What right do you have to sleep in my bed?"

"The right of your future husband. Now shut up and let me sleep for another hour. I got in at four this morning."

The phone shrilled just as he had said it would.

"That will be my driver. Tell him we won't be needing him this morning." He yawned.

Gena threw the light covers back and marched around the bed on her way to take a shower. "Tell him yourself!"

When she came out of the bathroom, he was gone. It surprised her a little. He had looked almost too tired to move, lying there in his shirt and pants. Four o'clock he had said. And then to get into bed with her! Especially after she had made it clear yesterday morning that she wanted nothing more to do with him.

She reached for a two-piece dress. Yesterday she had worn slacks to cover the long scratch on her lower leg, but today its redness was nearly gone. Her makeup was already applied, her long hair left loose so that it lay around her shoulders and halfway down her back, just touching the lace that edged the top of her slip, when Alex burst in, his face livid.

"Wha . . . what is it?" she stammered. In one hand he waved a newspaper, with the other he continued to retain a white-knuckled hold on the doorknob.

"According to this paper, Nick is married!"

Gena let both sections of the dress slip from her weakened fingers.

"I suppose you knew nothing about it?"

"No," she croaked.

Alex took a deep breath.

"This article says that he was joined in holy wedlock the night you arrived in Athens. Now think carefully before you answer, Gena. Did he or did he not meet you at the airport that night?"

"No," she repeated, this time reluctantly, "he didn't."

"So help me, I'll throttle him! I swear it!"

Gena gasped. She had never seen anyone so angry in her life. She clasped her hands together to prevent them from shaking.

"But Alex just because he didn't tell you . . ." She swallowed, seeing that his attention was now directed toward her. "I mean, surely Nick is old enough to marry."

"That is not the point." His voice was soft as he drew closer to her. "If something had happened to you . . ."

Gena sighed as he pressed his mouth to the tender flesh of her throat.

"Alex . . ."

His arms brought her closer as he straightened. "Why do you wear so many clothes . . . ?"

She protested softly, though to no avail, as his hands expertly removed her slip.

"You are beautiful . . . so very beautiful." One arm curved around her waist, then sank lower, to grip the fleshier mound of her buttocks, gradually edging her up to meet his own rock-hard form. "You make me forget everything else. . . ."

Gena thrilled to the ragged quality of his voice, and when his lips sought hers, she eagerly returned his kisses. On his instructions she removed his shirt. He slipped off her bra, arousing her to such a pitch that her spine arched and her head was thrown back in ecstasy. More kisses followed, making her rest weakly against him.

"I cannot wait any longer. You understand?"

"Yes," she moaned.

"Get in bed. I'll join you in a moment."

He saw her hesitation. His hands opened his belt . . . "I ache for you, you sweet witch."

Gena licked her lips. "You said we would wait. . . ."

"It won't work. I had to stay away from you all of yesterday. One more day like that and I'll go mad!"

When he came to her, she was turned on her right side, her eyes shut tightly. She loved him and she was to be his wife. And he was being so mysteriously tender with her. Dared she hope . . . ?

He laughed softly. "Nakedness is essential, my angel. Don't be ashamed. You're so beautiful, so very, very beautiful."

Gena felt his weight on the mattress behind her. A strong, gentle grip forced her to roll on her back. The same hand strayed briefly, massaging the tips of her breasts so that they became hard and sensitive. She kept her eyes closed.

"First I am a witch, now you call me an angel," she said. "You should make up your mind."

"Take off that dainty little undergarment and

you'll soon know what it is to be a woman. Or shall I?" He pulled them down slowly as if savoring every inch of her. Overcome, she looked away.

"Are you shy? Look at me."

"I can't."

His fingers trailed up her thigh. Her pulse went wild.

"Relax . . ."

"I . . . I can't," she gulped.

He began to touch her again, this time tracing invisible patterns on her cooling skin. His gentle touch acted as an erotic stimulus. She abandoned her previous inhibitions and allowed him to do whatever he pleased. Twice she reached a plateau of exquisite enjoyment. All the while he offered her quiet words of encouragement that seemed to increase her pleasure.

When his chest came down on her and his weight brought her further into the depths of the smooth sheets, she looked at him wildly, pushing against him.

"No. Someone will come. . . ." She panicked. "It's wrong. It's all wrong. I . . ."

His mouth silenced her. "There is no one here but us . . . my sweet wife-to-be."

She whimpered when his knee made its way between her tightly compressed legs, forcing them apart.

"You want this as much as I do, Gena. You wanted this when I first touched you. Just yesterday you were furious because I didn't take you. Believe me, I planned on waiting, but I can't turn back now.

147

I need you. I want you . . ." His words throbbed with desire.

"Please. Don't do this, Alex. . . . I—I'm scared!"

"I have to."

When his mouth covered hers again, she was lost. She clung tightly to him, forgetting her nervous fears in the ecstasy of the moment.

7

"Mother looked better today," Alex commented as they sat in the dim restaurant's most secluded corner.

"Yes. Her color is a lot better. It's good to know that she will be out of intensive care tomorrow." Gena blotted her mouth, then laid the napkin aside. "I just hope we're doing the right thing. It would be terrible if she found out about us. Before we choose to tell her, I mean. I hope we can tell her soon. How will I ever explain this?" She held up her left hand, flashing the ring he had given her just that evening. The central stone, a large glowing emerald, shimmered with an ethereal warmth. Its dazzling oval shape was surrounded by diamonds and set in gold. The ring fit as if it had been made for her. "You'll only be able to wear it when we're alone these next few weeks. I'll have to ask Mother's doctors for permission before I dare reveal what we feel for one another." He grimaced slightly. "Speaking of doctors reminds me that Kostas is being sent home today. He will be hobbling about for a month or two. That will teach him to behave for a while. Come, I want you to have an early night. After all, tomorrow afternoon you become my wife."

"Alex?" They were nearing the tall, familiar building owned by the man who was now her husband. He slowed and braked, turning into the parking area.

"You sound serious. . . ."

She had to ask. "What about . . . Sofia?"

He looked at her in astonishment. "I hope you don't think that I'm seeing her. Since you, there has been no one." His look darkened. "I considered myself wedded to you from the first time I took you. For me, today's ceremony was a mere formality, protecting your reputation, binding you to *me*, should you become pregnant!" In a lower, gentler tone he added, "Sofia filled a need—a sexual need. Don't worry about her. I arranged for her to move to London. She hopes for a singing career."

"I didn't mean to pry." Gena plucked at the cream material of her dress.

"Your opinion of me is not a very flattering one. Why on earth would I marry you and continue to bed *her*?" he wondered aloud.

"I couldn't help but wonder. You never said a word."

He lit a cheroot as they continued to sit and talk. "What bride likes to hear herself compared to another woman? Or are you different?"

"You . . . once told me you only like experienced women. . . ."

"I was bluffing, thinking that saying it could somehow make it true. I am proud to be your first lover." He blew some smoke in her direction. "And if you know what's good for you . . . I shall also be your last."

Once inside the apartment, their passion flung them into each other's arms. Hungrily, they kissed, and his strong hands began to remove all barriers between them. Her dress slipped to the floor. His eyes strayed to the creamy breasts that were partly visible over the lace of her slip and its matching flesh-colored bra.

"Dear Lord, but you are beautiful. . . ." His voice shuddered with his deep emotion.

They were so thoroughly involved in one another that they did not observe Nick's arrival until it was too late.

Gena was the first to see him. A panicky, breathless instant passed before she could convey her sense of shock to Alex.

"Darling, what is it?" he asked hoarsely. "Have I hurt you?"

She managed to shake her head. "It's Nick . . . Nick is here," she choked out. Her nervous hands reached for the slip and dress that Alex had impatiently tugged aside.

Alex at once turned to face his brother, who was gaping at them in disbelief. "You dirty swine! Get away from her!" Nick lashed out suddenly, while Alex moved to shield Gena from his view.

"Nick, I refuse to fight you. Let me explain."

Alex stopped talking as a fist grazed his chin. He tried grabbing for it, but Nick was faster.

"Stop it!" Gena sobbed, looking around Alex's right shoulder. "We're married!"

"The devil you are!"

"What Gena said is true. We were wed this afternoon."

"You can't marry your own niece!"

Alex blocked the next blow by raising an arm.

"I'm not your niece. Not yours, not Alex's. Not in the real sense. I was adopted."

Nick took a step backward. "But Ava—she was with child. . . . How . . . ?"

"Her natural daughter died just after birth. She never knew I was substituted." Gena continued to look at the thunderstruck Nick with compassion. Alex's arms gathered her close against his chest.

"When did *he* find out?" he asked, pointing at Alex.

"The first night that I arrived on the island." She lowered her voice to a whisper. "You see, I had just found out a few weeks before . . . by accident. Father could never bring himself to tell me. He was afraid that I would end up hating him." She felt Alex's protective arms tighten around her waist. "But he finally told me everything. . . ."

"No one else knows," Alex put in quietly, "and we prefer to keep it that way until Mother is well enough. You understand."

"It is incredible." Nick ran a hand through his dark wavy hair. "I don't know what to say." He looked embarrassed. "May I offer my congratulations?" After an awkward pause, he went on. "I only stopped by to invite you both to meet my wife on Sunday. It seems we never see each other any more—just in passing at the hospital." Another pause. "I want you to meet her."

Gena answered for both of them. "I'm sure we'll be happy to. But, for now . . ."

Goodbyes were quickly said.

"Must you look so handsome?" She eyed the white three-piece suit Alex wore. A black, open-necked shirt completed the totally devastating picture, while a gold medallion mingled with the crisp, dark hair on his upper chest. "The first thing I'm going to do is check out your secretary," she warned him, placing his breakfast on the kitchen table as he entered the room.

"My private secretary happens to be a man. If lilias were introduced to you, he would go mad. Therefore, I shall keep you safely tucked from sight until I can declare to the world that you are mine." He kissed her, then sat down to eat.

"I hope you don't mind cooking for me. Or

keeping the place tidy. I gave my housekeeper another few weeks vacation." His eyes smiled across at her as she stirred the sugar and cream into her coffee. "Being alone with you is very important to me. I want no restraints placed on our relationship at this point. There are enough problems to be resolved."

"I would do anything you wanted, Alex. You know that." Her cheeks were flushed with feeling. Their hands met and clung.

"Yes," he said softly. "And if I didn't have appointments set up for this morning, I would be here with you. You know that. When I am away from you, my mind wanders. I find myself . . . agitated . . . aroused by my recollections of you."

As they kissed goodbye, Gena said, "I think I'll go to the hospital this morning, then do a little shopping. I *would* like a new dress for Sunday."

"Buy ten."

"Alex!"

He laughed. "Darling, you can have whatever you like. I told you before that money is no problem. Wherever you go, have the owner or shopkeeper phone me at this number." He jotted down a phone number on a small card and handed it to her. "My secretary will verify that your charges will be paid, and"—he drew a money clip from his pocket, pressing at least half of its contents into her palm—"that should take care of any trinkets or scarves or your lunch."

"This will take care of my lunches for a year!"

"Shh," he warned, teasingly. "I have to have

some reason for supplying you with cash. I shall inform Spiros that he is driving you." They kissed once more. "This afternoon. At two." He pointed to the steps. "You be up there, waiting," he growled, then left.

Gena's heart swelled with emotion. Life was wonderful. He must love her, he must. No man could speak so tenderly to a woman—to his wife— and not love her. If only he would say the words. Perhaps this afternoon . . . ?

It was one-thirty. Gena tossed four dress boxes on the satin coverlet, glad to be able to sink down beside them and shed her shoes. Her shopping had been fun, but tiring. On Alex's specific instructions, the willing Spiros had driven her to two exclusive women's apparel showrooms, one on Nikis Street, the other located on Lisou. There were still several items to be delivered from both shops—she had really outdone herself. Still, she felt guilty; she had spent so little time at the hospital. A few minutes after Gena's arrival, Madame Andreas had drifted off into a restful slumber and, according to her private nurse, she would not awaken for some time. Gena had gone on her way, leaving behind a reminder of her visit—a bouquet of flowers and a cheery note.

She pressed a hand to her complaining stomach. Its gurgling noises reminded her that she had forgotten to have lunch. Rather than trudge downstairs, Gena decided to undress and take a refreshing bath. She would eat later.

A favorite tune was on her lips as she sat, brushing the thick waves of her freshly shampooed, blow-dried hair. Alex's dresser mirror reflected her glowing, healthy complexion. A smile curved the corners of her mouth.

Gena felt excitement stir deep inside her. Alex would be back soon. She wore his robe—it was all she had on. She rubbed a cheek against its soft shawl collar, allowing her arms to rest for a moment. The robe had his clean male fragrance. Knowing that Alex had worn it this morning after taking his shower made her pulse quicken. If he were here with her right now, there was little doubt in her mind as to what they would be doing. Gena hugged the soft towelling fabric all the closer and wished for his swift return.

Her eyes darted to the half-open door. What was that? She rose to listen. When she heard the sound again, her lips curved into a knowing smile.

It had to be Alex. He must have forgotten his key. Gena streaked down the hall in her bare feet; her racing steps took her down the steps toward the main entrance.

But when she flung the door open, instead of greeting her husband, she came face to face with a sober-looking Kostas! He rested on a pair of crutches. Gena's eager smile dimmed and vanished. "What do you want?" she demanded. Her hands fumbled to tighten the robe's loose front.

"May I come in?" he asked in a contrite tone.

The man had gall. "Certainly not!" After all he had put her through?

"I came to apologize. The drinks . . . they must have gone to my head. I swear by the gods . . . I do not know what came over me."

Gena forced herself to exhibit a calm exterior, but inside she was panicky. Where was Spiros? Surely, Alex must have told him that Kostas was not welcome in his household?

She jumped nervously as Kostas lurched a step closer.

"Five minutes, Gena. That is all I ask. Must we stand out here and talk?" He motioned to his cast.

"I only wish I had pushed you harder!"

His startled gaze moved over her angry, flushed features. "I believe you truly mean that."

"You bet I do." A quick step to the rear provided her with the extra inch she needed to slam the door in his face.

"You thought I would be late, so you invited him here!" His eyes had never looked blacker.

Gena flinched. "Alex, you can't really mean that!" Didn't he know how much she loved him?

"What made you do it? Am I not man enough for you?" he raged, pacing the bedroom. She sat on the edge of the bed, still wearing his robe. Not even five minutes had elapsed since Kostas' departure. Alex had seen him being helped into his limousine as he had pulled up in his own car.

As she began to speak again, his arms reached for her, but instead of gathering her close, he shook her. The robe parted, displaying her nakedness.

"Alex, please believe me," she pleaded, knowing what he must be thinking. "I thought it was you. . . ." Gena cried out in agony as he grabbed the thick hair that swung freely around her shoulders and pulled her head back.

"Is every man the same to you? Do I look like Kostas?" His eyes blazed into her face, his anger like nothing she had ever experienced before. "Did he please you? Tell me, Gena. Is he as good in bed as I am?"

What was he saying . . . what terrible things was he accusing her of?

The robe was jerked from her shoulders. Gena felt it cover her bare toes as it fell to the carpet. When she tried to cover herself with crossed arms, he ordered her to get into the bed.

"Alex?" she whispered, not believing what was happening.

He began to undress, then seeing that she had not obeyed him, he pushed her so that she fell onto the slippery spread.

"What makes women like you tick, I wonder?" His face was devoid of expression as he threw his shirt to the floor. "Helene was the same type, but at least she had the decency to wait until the honeymoon was over."

Gena moved to the far side of the bed and lay there, numb. He was going to punish her. "Don't . . . please don't. I love you. Only you," she pleaded, even as his weight moved the bed.

At first she had struggled, but on seeing the cruelty that was reflected in his black eyes, she eventually turned a cheek into the pillow beneath her head and waited until his punishing body had finished with her. She kept her eyes closed until he lifted himself away. Shame flooded through her as she remembered how her weak body had responded to him despite her efforts to stay still in the face of his passion.

He kept his back to her as he dressed. "The only thing I shall require of you is the use of your body from time to time."

"Alex . . . let me explain." Her voice was a whisper, thick with tears.

He turned to face her, his face contorted with rage. "I do not want to hear any more lies, do you hear?" he shouted. "What do you take me for—an idiot?"

Gena did not have the strength to fight him any longer.

Just before he slammed the bedroom door, he ordered her to move back into her own room. "And if I do not visit your bed with regular frequency," he finished, "it will indicate that I seek my pleasures elsewhere!"

They didn't go to Nick's apartment as planned. She overheard Alex excusing them from the commitment as he spoke to his brother over the phone, citing their desire to be alone for a while longer. What a joke! She was Alex's prisoner, allowed out only to visit his mother and only while in his company.

A week dragged by, then another. Their relationship did not improve. She had given up trying to explain her meeting with Kostas.

The worst test for her control always came on the rare occasions when Alex came to her bed. She tried keeping her body tense, so that she wouldn't reciprocate and meet his demands willingly, but her body always betrayed her, responding to him with a passion she could not hide. The darkness of her bedroom helped to hide the tears that fell as he took what was legally his.

One day, late in August, Gena rolled out of bed at her usual time to prepare their breakfast, only to grope dizzily for the edge of the bedside table to steady herself. The uneasy feeling lasted until early afternoon.

It happened again the next morning, and the next. What kind of a bug had she picked up? she wondered on the third day while dragging herself around the apartment to finish what little house-work the cleaning woman left for her.

She made herself a sandwich, then ate it while writing a letter to her father. The bread almost made her choke, but she forced herself to finish the last of the grilled cheese. Her appetite had waned, though Alex had paid no attention. He was never at the apartment long enough to notice anything; she rarely saw him. He usually ate his evening meal out.

Gena headed for the bath, her shoulders droop-ing. She couldn't blame her problem on Alex. He hadn't come near her for five days. Her smile was bitter. It was now quite obvious that his need of her had been diverted to another woman's body.

She had one foot in the tub when the realization struck her. As she lowered her shivering form into the enveloping warmth, she gave a low moan. Her body felt strangely feverish and cold as ice.

"Please . . . no," she murmured. Alex, oh, Alex . . . He must never know; she had to get away somehow. But where . . . and how? In a few months it would be too late. She laid a hand to her stomach. Having Alex's child would be heaven and hell—just like living with him. An exhilarating feeling seemed to surge suddenly inside her, despite her desperate misgivings about being pregnant. She was actually going to have a baby—Alex's baby. And it *had* been conceived in love; she must believe that. She counted on her fingers. Yes. It might even have been the first time they had made love. At least she had *that* to remember.

She washed herself slowly, thinking and planning all the while. There were bus routes as well as a connection by the underground line that serviced Kifissia. If she was going to get away, she would have to move quickly, preferably in the next two days. Alex's mother—it was hard to think of her as her grandmother anymore, she found, despite the fact that their marriage was still a secret—was to be taken back to the island the day after tomorrow and they would all be returning with her. Alex had not said so, of course, but she could only assume that she would be going along.

There was still plenty of money, both Greek and American, in her purse. At last glance her passport was still safely stashed in it, as was her return ticket to New York, a ticket she had begun to think she would never use. All she had to do was get to Hellenikon Airport. . . .

It would be necessary to tell her father who, as yet, had no idea that she had married Alex. There was no other way. She swallowed hard, trying to keep back the tears. Facing him would be the hardest thing of all; fathers always seemed to think of their daughters as little girls—and she knew that her own was no exception. But first things first.

She stepped from the tub, drying herself briskly.

In exactly one hour Alex would be arriving to drive her to the hospital. Since that was the only outing she expected, she would prepare herself just in case she could get away. Who knew whether or not she would even be going there tomorrow?

She dressed carefully, donning a pale linen suit, its light tan color brilliantly accented by a deep purple silk blouse. They were both new. Everything else would have to stay here, she decided. And that included the ring he had bought her. And the gold wedding band. He could have it all back. She sniffed a little, holding back her tears.

Her hair was in a top knot. Tiny amethyst earrings pierced her ear lobes, matching the birth-stone ring given to her by her father. The shoes she wore were of cream leather; she had bought them to match the suit. They were a little higher heeled than she was accustomed to wearing, but they were comfortable.

Before leaving her bedroom, she gripped the doorknob for a moment before resolutely closing the door behind her. There was no time for second thoughts. Not now. The only thing that mattered was getting home to New York. If only New York still *were* home, but only Greece, and Alex, were home to her now.

Her high heels traversed the long hall quickly, making barely a sound as they connected with the tufted carpeting. The steps soon loomed below. Had she heard a door closing? For a brief moment, the tan carpeted steps blurred as her head swam.

"What's wrong with you?" a voice called sharply.

Gena swallowed. Alex was approaching from below. He placed a hand on the staircase, waiting for her reply. With an assuredness of manner that she did not really feel, Gena waved a casual hand, then let it drop to her leather shoulderbag. She gripped the balustrade with her right hand.

"Nothing is wrong. I was just coming down." She blinked, trying desperately to shake the funny feeling she was still experiencing. To gain herself more time, she announced in a bright voice, "I didn't really expect you for another half hour." He swung about, walking in the direction of his den. If only . . .

His spiteful words cut into her wishful thinking. "Did you hope to put in a call to your lover?"

Gena's sharp, delicately enamelled nails dug into the polished wood that graced the curved railing. She pressed her lips together and took a shaky step, but as she did so her left heel caught on a loop in the rug, making her lose her precarious balance. A scream rose in her throat and caught there as her body tumbled head over heels. . . .

A serious-faced woman was bent over her, one hand firmly fastened on her wrist when she awakened. She was lying down in a strange room.

"I... must get up," she panicked. "Please..."

"You must rest, miss." Two hands now held her down.

"I . . . can't!" Gena moved restlessly, attempting to escape the confining pressure. "I have to go home." She licked her dry lips. "My father will worry," she croaked. "He doesn't like me out late. He worries so much."

"It's still early," the soothing voice assured her. "You'll be home on time."

Gena closed her eyes and relaxed.

The English-speaking nurse turned to address the man who had been pacing the private room as if possessed. He now stood frozen at the foot of the bed in the room's early evening shadows.

"Your niece appears to be disoriented, sir. However, when she comes around again, there should be an improvement. Her system has suffered a shock." Then, taking pity on the man's agitation, she said, "I'll be back shortly. Will you stay until I return?" She knew he would, of course. "I must inform her doctor that she has awakened."

He dismissed her with a wave of his hand, not trusting himself to speak.

"Gena . . . darling, I am sorry." He hadn't meant to speak. Her eyes fluttered, then opened.

"Alex?" she asked. "Wha . . . what are you doing here? Where am I?" She looked around in confusion, noting, as if for the first time, the strange appearance of the room.

"In a hospital. You fell."

Gena stared at him for a full minute. "Yes. I remember now," she stated dully. "Did you bring me here?"

"I did," he acknowledged.

"Why?"

He looked at her helplessly for a minute, not knowing how to answer. "You fell," he repeated quietly.

"Wouldn't it have been easier just to leave me . . . as you found me?" she asked coldly, turning her head to look at the apricot wall. "Did I lose the baby?" Her voice was flat; he undoubtedly knew by now. When there was no immediate answer to her question, she looked at him again. He had his back to her. "Well?"

Alex took a deep breath, trying to keep his voice steady. His hands shook. He stuffed them into his pockets.

"Yes." His voice slashed the stillness with its tortured admission.

Gena curled a hand over the top of the sheet that covered her chest. "I'm glad," she taunted. "Nothing binds us then. I can return to New York free and clear of you." She tried to laugh, but it came out sounding like a ragged sob. "There won't be an embarrassing bulge to explain now. I was going to make my escape today . . . you didn't know that, did you? I had everything ready—my passport, money. . . . Daddy was so right about you. He warned me, Alex, but I didn't pay attention." The violet eyes looked at him wildly. "You never loved me. It was all such a sham," she moaned. "You never once told me that you loved me. . . ." A hand dropped to her stomach, as if she were in pain. "Get out of my sight. I never want to see you again. . . ." She was fast becoming hysterical. "Never . . . never!"

Just then, the nurse rushed across the threshold, visibly concerned about Gena's welfare. Her voice had penetrated into the hallway of the private clinic.

After convincing her sobbing patient to accept a pill that would calm her anxieties and make her sleep, the nurse turned to say a few words to the tall, silent man who had brought her to the emergency room in the early afternoon, but he was gone.

Strange. He had been there a moment ago. She had only wanted to tell him that his niece wasn't herself yet. It would take time. Losing a baby wasn't the easiest thing to accept.

While she waited for the young woman's eyes to close and for the doctor to come, she glanced at the smooth hand that held no wedding band, sighing. A pity. It was no wonder that her uncle, a man known throughout the world, had chosen to entrust her to Dr. Theo's private care.

8

·∞∞∞∞∞∞∞∞∞.

Gena poured herself a little more apple cider, looking around the decorated room in satisfaction.

"How does this look?" her father called, stretching to place a glittering star atop the Christmas tree.

"A little more to the left, I think." Gena wrinkled her nose at his initial attempt. She sipped her drink, then nodded. "That's fine." She watched as he stepped down off the wooden chair. "Doesn't it look nice?"

He agreed. "I'm glad we decided on a real tree this year." He breathed in deeply, then put an arm around her shoulder. "What a smell. It reminds me of the Christmas visits to my grandmother's years ago when I was just a little kid." James felt her tense. It had happened several times before when he had come to stand close to her, or given her a happy hug. He took a deep breath, determined to find the cause of her coolness toward any sign of affection. She had been like this ever since coming back from her trip to Greece. Something had happened over there, and he was going to find out one way or another what it was.

"What's wrong, baby?" he asked quietly. "You just don't seem like my little girl anymore." He thought a moment, then dropped his arm and moved away. "Is it something I've done? Are you upset because of your adoption, is that it?" He had to start somewhere.

Gena shook her head, pushing the short, dark hair off her forehead. She'd had it cut a few days after getting back home. Its heaviness had suddenly irritated her.

"Don't mind me, Dad. I'm just moody, I guess." She went to stare out the window, looking down at the blazing holiday lights.

James sighed heavily. He was getting nowhere. "All right, don't tell me. It isn't any of my business anyway." Then, "Are you going to sign up for classes next semester?"

"I might."

"Gena . . ."

"Dad, *please.*" There were tears in her voice.

"Do you want to finish putting the icicles on the tree?" He picked up the chair, heading for the kitchen.

"Sure," she replied. "In a minute. You go on to bed; I can tidy up."

"Don't forget that we have a date next Saturday night," he called cheerfully.

"I promise to be ready," she said, though without any noticeable enthusiasm.

Once the room was back in order, Gena finished decorating the tree, painstakingly placing one silver, shimmering icicle every inch or so until the prickly branches glittered from her patient efforts. She deliberately concentrated on what she was doing, sometimes unconsciously humming along with the holiday tunes on the radio.

She was on her knees again, straining to reach a bright red velvet ornament that had fallen down, when the low, smooth tones of a traditional carol penetrated her hearing, filling her throat with a lump that made swallowing difficult. One raw sob turned into two. She just couldn't bear to listen to it any longer. In seconds, she was on her feet and racing to push the "off" button, one hand still clutching the Christmas ball.

For her father's peace of mind, she knew she had to pull herself together. She knew he was worried about her. And yet, she couldn't help the way she felt. The last three months had been torture. Wasn't she ever going to forget? Wasn't the pain going to ease at all?

The four days she had spent in Dr. Theopolous' clinic had passed in a blur, but she remembered the following week with a pain that refused to be exorcised. Nick and his English wife, Molly, had insisted that she convalesce at their apartment when Alex had taken it upon himself to inform them of their strained relations. Since that first afternoon, he had not contacted her in any way. Nick had driven her to the airport and seen her off.

Her face crumpled. She had trouble sleeping . . . she was losing weight. By summer she was going to look like a walking skeleton if her weight loss continued. Another pound had vanished last week. She made her way back to the tree to rehang the fallen ornament.

Gena knew that her bitterness toward Alex was a thing of the past, buried in the love she still felt for him. She constantly wondered what he was doing. She and Nick's wife often exchanged letters, but there was never a mention of Alex in any of them. Her lips compressed. It was inevitable that he would have taken another mistress by now.

The New York skyline beckoned again. "Beautiful," she whispered, trying desperately to banish the thought of another woman's body lying next to his. It was nearly one o'clock. She soon shut the drapes and touched the light switch. The last one up always put things in order.

"How do I look?"

"Utterly beautiful."

Gena twirled in front of the Christmas tree, its blinking lights catching the dull sheen of her long black gown. Its skirt swirled around her legs, wrapping itself around her trim ankles, showing off the delicate shoes she wore. She felt elegant.

"You don't think it's too low in front?"

Her father looked at her in astonishment. "You're covered up to your neck!"

"But it's sheer." She nibbled a glossy lip. "Should I change? Be honest, Dad." The fine, see-through fabric that fitted snugly over her arms to her wrists also dropped to display the curve of her breasts, causing her some concern.

"You look just fine. Now close your eyes. I have a surprise."

Something long and warm was draped over her shoulders.

"I think I'm going to cry." she said, running her hand along the beautiful sable coat.

"You've been doing too much of that lately." His tone was firm. "Starting tonight, I want you to enjoy life again."

The sounds of laughter and the clinking of glasses could be heard as a uniformed maid took their coats in the foyer. A piano provided background music.

"Ready, pet?" Her father offered his arm. He was so proud of her tonight; she looked so lovely. She was perfection from the top of her glossy, dark hair to the slender feet encased in shining black leather pumps. Tiny diamond studs pierced her ears. A diamond teardrop nestled on its silver chain around her neck.

"What would you like to drink?"

"White wine would be nice." They were standing near the curved bar which was manned by two young men in white jackets. "Alice is drifting over. She's seen us."

"I'm sure she's kept one eye on the doorway. I really didn't give her a firm confirmation." He handed Gena her drink.

"Oh? Why not?"

"I wasn't too sure how you felt about going out. You have to admit you haven't been in the best of spirits lately." He broke off as both host and hostess approached.

"Gena, you look absolutely gorgeous," the petite redhead exclaimed, standing on tiptoes to kiss her cheek. "Doesn't she Jeremy?"

"Absolutely!" said Mr. Fielding's first assistant and right-hand man, raising his drink. "Happy holidays to one and all." He grinned and adjusted his red tie. "See what she made me wear? I feel like Kris Kringle himself." He motioned them to follow him. "Come on. Let's find a spot to sit and talk. There's plenty of room on the sofa near the piano." He raised his voice as merry laughter broke out from a group of people not far from them. "What do you think, James? Alice did herself proud, wouldn't you say?"

The piano playing grew louder as they climbed the four steps that led to the upper area. Just as Gena was about to take a seat next to her father, someone called her name over the din. She looked around curiously. "In back of you," the voice instructed.

"Rich! Rich Blackman! How are you?" She was pleased to see someone she knew. "Are you still working at the U.N.?" He had been one of the language translators there.

He grinned, showing his perfect white teeth. "Yes."

Gena was well aware that her father was listening. She introduced them. "How is it that you got an invitation?"

"Alice is my cousin." His brown eyes danced. "Actually, I crashed this shindig because I knew you were coming."

Gena regarded him with a cynical smile. She was one of the few who had held out against his wolfish charm.

He cocked his blond head and threw a meaningful glance at the lone couple swaying to the music on the far side of the piano. "How about it?"

Because her father was half-listening to their banter, she turned to seek approval from him. "He isn't asking *me* to dance, dear," was his wry comment.

"Alice has a thing about romantic music," Rich mouthed somewhere in the vicinity of her right ear as they danced slowly across the floor.

Gena wanted to cry out "So do I," but the words stuck in her throat. She and Alex had danced on their wedding night. At home. When the slow waltz was only half over he had begun to undress her, then urged her to do the same to him. The thick salon carpet had become their bed as he had proceeded to make sensual love to her. The memory was so shattering that she stumbled against Rich.

"Excuse me," she managed to gasp out.

"My pleasure."

Gena stopped dancing. "I didn't do that on purpose," she stated coolly.

"A guy can hope, can't he?" He grinned, undaunted.

When she declined to dance anymore, he led her back toward her seat.

His hand spread itself in the center of her back, guiding her as they threaded their way past some late arrivals. By the time Gena returned to her father's side, her head was swimming. Rich must have introduced her to a dozen people, most of whom had taken it for granted that they were a couple. Gena tensed as he perched on the arm of the blue velvet sofa, just a few inches from her.

She glanced at her father. Why had she ever consented to attend Alice's party? She sighed and wished her father didn't appear to be having such a good time. He was laughing and talking with an attractive woman on his right. She took a swallow of her wine and then carefully placed the glass on a tray.

"Where are you off to?" Rich inquired in surprise.

"The powder room," she lied. Gena didn't want him following her; she had to be alone for a while. The milling, party-minded crowd and the wine she had consumed, not to mention Rich's persistent friendliness, were all contributing to her growing tension.

A festively decorated open doorway beckoned, and she soon found herself walking down a path of mint green carpeting. Gena counted five closed doors in the hallway before crossing over to choose the nearest one.

The room was exactly what she had hoped to find, a cozy den. Inside, a small desk lamp burned, allowing her the luxury of not having to search for a light switch. She picked up a novel and sat down.

A soprano's voice, high and clear, seeped into the room. Gena lost interest in the novel and listened to the rendition of a famous Christmas carol, allowing the book to close and slip down by her side. When the song was finished, Gena realized that she was too moved to leave the confines of the den just yet, though she wanted to find her father and ask him to bring her home. She brushed a tear from the corner of an eye.

"There you are!"

She looked up quickly, to see her father standing in the open door. "Daddy, could we go now?" she choked out, looking at him.

"Honey, what's wrong? Are you ill?" He rushed to her.

"I'm not feeling . . . right," she admitted.

"Shall I call a doctor?"

"Medicine won't help," she told him wearily, fingering the binding on the book.

"Don't you think it's time we had that talk? You and I both know something is wrong."

"You wouldn't understand." Her chin quivered and she bowed her head to hide its movement.

"Gena, I'd bet my right arm that there's a man involved. Why, any fool could see that you're heartbroken!" He touched her shoulder, then looked over the back of the sofa as a dull glint caught his attention. A man stepped out of the gloom where he had been hidden and into the dusky light.

James met Alex's steady gaze. Everything made sense at last; he got to his feet. "Alice should be told we're leaving."

"I'll come with you." She still hadn't seen the man standing in the shadows behind her.

"No. Stay where you are. I'll be back." His last few words were meant to warn the other man.

"Gena . . ."

She stiffened, her violet eyes shimmering with uncertainty. Had she imagined that someone—no, not someone, Alex—had called her name? The tortured sound had come from behind her, or so it had seemed. Almost fearfully, she turned to look.

Jet eyes glittered, trapping her in their depths. There was a trembling in her legs that refused to stop. Gena reaced up to touch her forehead in confusion. "Alex . . . ?"

"Your hair—you've had it cut," he said, drawing closer. He reached out to touch the short, smooth waves. Gena bowed her head to meet his fingers, and as she did so, she closed her eyes and breathed in the tangy smell of cheroot smoke that clung to him. His hand trailed over a heated cheekbone, and when it brushed her parted mouth, she responded to its caress by kissing it, moistening his fingertips with her tongue, tasting his flesh. . . .

Within moments she was in his arms. They clung

to one another, each meeting and matching the passion that mounted in the other's body.

"Alex . . . Alex," she sobbed. "You've no idea how much I've longed to have you hold me like this. . . . I've missed you so much. . . ."

"Kiss me . . . !"

As their lips met, Gena thrilled to the intimate pressure of his thighs moving seductively against her. She did not have to be told to respond; she longed to touch him. Her fingers spread over the warm, muscled skin of his back after slipping beneath his fine wool sweater, and as the material pulled loose in the front, she did not hesitate to rub her hands over the crisp dark hairs that covered his chest.

"I love you," he repeated over and over again as his lips explored the hollows of her ears and neck, while his hands massaged and stroked her. . . . Through love-glazed eyes she watched as his dark head dipped lower.

A cry wrenched itself from within her as his hands cupped her full breasts. He kissed them reverently, then raised his head, saying hoarsely, "We will both be sick if I continue this . . . torture." He looked into her passion-glazed eyes. "Your father will be returning, too." He drew a steadying breath and the embrace that followed was gentle.

"We have so much to talk about, so much to tell one another," she whispered, content in his arms.

"Later," he promised, his hold on her tightening. "But I must know if you can ever forgive me. My jealousy was inexcusable. Instead of believing you, trusting you, I punished you for something you weren't guilty of, destroying your happiness—and mine." He shuddered against her. "How could I have been so cruel, so inhuman? You were little more than a child," he agonized.

"I? A child?" she scoffed, trying to lift him out of his dark mood. *"Kyrie, that would be like calling you a mere boy!"* She saw the question in his eyes. "I forgave you long ago, my love."

"This time, *woman*," he emphasized, "I won't let you out of my sight."

Gena smiled. The familiar arrogance had returned. She stretched on tiptoes to kiss him. "Lovely."

"Come." He motioned to the sofa behind them. "Let us sit and talk. I have a few things that belong to you."

They were conversing quietly when the knock came. Her wedding rings glittered on her hand as she nervously fingered the chain at her neckline. "I must look a mess."

"You look loved," Alex said, just before he opened the door to admit his father-in-law.

179

9

Gena lay in the circle of her husband's arms. It was approaching two o'clock, a new day, a new beginning.

"Your father seemed happy for us," Alex commented softly against the top of her head.

A low light burned next to the bed in their Waldorf-Astoria suite. Alex had insisted that it remain on so he could feast his eyes on her naked perfection.

"I'm so glad you were with me when I told him." Gena lifted on one elbow to stare down into the face of her beloved husband.

"Are you glad I followed you?"

"Ecstatic! But how did you find us?"

"I arrived at your apartment earlier this evening. It couldn't have been too long after you and James had gone. So I checked in at this hotel, had some decent food sent up, and then made my way to the party."

"But—how would you have found me? What if I hadn't gone into the study?" She stopped, too afraid to face the thought that they might never have met again.

Alex shook his head, sighing. "I didn't want to greet you with a crowd of people around us. If you want to know the truth, I was hiding until I got my courage up. I was going to give one of the maids a note to slip to you, then have you meet me in that very room. When I saw you . . ."

"It's a good thing the housekeeper was home," she said thoughtfully, "or you might never have found me."

"I would have waited on your doorstep."

"You should have come weeks and weeks ago, darling."

"How could I? Knowing that you never wanted to see me again . . . that you hated me?"

"I barely remember the awful things I said to you at the clinic. I was so groggy . . . confused."

"We'll live on the island for most of the year. Do you mind?" he asked, after a few moments of contemplative silence.

"I can't think of a more beautiful place," she replied, her violet eyes reflecting her happiness. To her, it was paradise.

"When you . . . left Greece I got rid of the apartment in Kifissia." When she did not comment, he continued, "Instead, I shall have a small villa built for us on the coast, not far from Athens. It will be our private residence when we are on the mainland. Is this agreeable to you?"

He sounds almost anxious, she thought. "Of course, darling." Gena felt the tension leave his body. "Did you doubt for a moment that I would return to Greece with you?" She lifted the hand that was resting across her stomach toward her face, cradling it against one cheek. "If you told me that we would be sheltered by a single palm tree . . . or two boards nailed together . . . a blanket of stars above us, it wouldn't matter," she told him. "There are times I've wished you weren't so important. . . ." Her voice ended in a gasp as the hand she had been holding slid down past her throat to tantalize her breasts. Within moments her breathing grew agitated. Gena knew that her husband was well aware of her arousal, even though he chose not to do anything about it just yet. He seemed to derive a great deal of pleasure from watching her expressive face.

"You have such lovely skin. It was one of the first things I noticed about you." A gentle push brought her back so that she lay flat. "You taste like cream and feel like silk," he said.

Gena moaned and shivered at the same time. He had spread his hand over her soft breast, teasing the rosy crown until it seemed to beg for the touch of his hard mouth. Her eyes closed.

"Why are you torturing me like this?" she managed to ask.

"Don't you like it?" he asked in a husky voice.

"Yes . . . but . . ."

"Talk to me."

"How . . . how can I?" she breathed. "When you touch me, I can't even *think* coherently!" Her skin felt as if it was on fire. She kicked at the covers, then pushed them past her ankles.

Finally she felt the circular, massaging motion cease. His hard, hot flesh rubbed her side.

"Now you know how I feel about you—every time you are near—or when we are apart. I couldn't think straight when I saw Kostas leaving our apartment."

His sudden reference to that day made Gena understand how much he still agonized over it. "Nothing happened," she whispered, seeing the tortured look on his face.

"I know that."

Gena sat up, at the same time pushing a lock of dark hair from her flushed cheek.

"You . . . didn't ask him?" The very thought of such a conversation made her sick.

"There was no need to."

"What do you mean?"

"When I made love to you, I knew my accusations were false, that you were telling the truth, but my pride wouldn't allow me to admit that I had been wrong."

Gena's skin felt chilled now and her senses were returning to normal. Because she had loved him then, as now, she felt confused by his statement.

"But . . . if you could tell that I hadn't been unfaithful, why did you continue to treat me as if I had?"

"The angrier I became with myself, the more I took it out on you," he answered in a tight, withdrawn tone. "It was a vicious circle. I couldn't work . . . or sleep. All I could think of was you, lying in your bed, in the room next to mine. I wanted to be with you, to confess that I loved you, but when I would push open your door at night and see the fear with which you greeted me, my fury at your rejection would override any tender, loving feelings inside me."

"No matter what you thought, I looked forward to those visits," she told him quietly. "At least then I felt alive. Later, I assumed you had taken a mistress."

His lips twisted. "I suppose you wish that I had."

Gena twisted around to face him more squarely. She began to shiver. "How could you say such a thing?" she choked out. Pain slashed through her, an emotional hurt so great that she felt as if someone had stabbed her with a knife.

He acted quickly when he saw that she was going to slip off the bed. One foot was already on the floor when he grabbed her. "Am I still so important?" he mocked, pressing her into the mound of rumpled blankets at the foot of the bed.

A tear slid out of the corner of one eye and into the hair near her temple. "Alex . . ."

"Love me . . . just love me," he groaned.

* * *

Their coming-together was both wild and beautiful.

A little later they soaped one another in the shower, laughing when their slippery bodies refused to remain in contact as they shared a quick embrace. Dry and clean again, they drew up the silky sheets and reached out to warm each other in the bed.

The room was dark, but their eyes soon became accustomed to it. Gena moved so that she could look up at his chiselled profile. It had been no easy task to convince him of the fact that she was willing to forgive his cruel words.

"Alex, would you really have seduced me in your room at the villa?"

He stirred and thought for a moment. "Probably," he answered in a throaty, tired voice.

"But you didn't know for sure that we weren't related. You only had my word."

"I had no choice but to believe you. By that time, my thoughts were hardly avuncular. Working on the yacht all that day, I fantasized about you. I couldn't keep my mind off you."

"You thought I was pregnant!" she bubbled.

"If you had been, I'd have married you anyway."

She rewarded him with a kiss. "Would you mind if I got pregnant right away? It might have happened already."

Gena saw his eyes flame. "I would like nothing better, though it is up to you. The wife should have *some* say in the matter, don't you agree?"

She stared at him, taking a moment to recognize the laughing glint in his eyes. "I suppose now you'll be telling me that you would like me to give you a son?"

"A daughter will be just fine," he chuckled. "Or two . . . or three."

"Did I hear you correctly in the taxi when you said you had told Ana and your mother?"

"You did. Mother cried because she was so happy, and Ana . . . do you know what she asked? She demanded to know just how many brothers and sisters she could count on having. She is already picking out names."

"Then we mustn't disappoint her," Gena breathed huskily, as she turned once more into the circle of his arms.

Silhouette Desire

Six new titles are published on the first Friday every month. All are available at your local bookshop or newsagent, so make sure of obtaining your copies by taking note of the following dates:

APRIL 1st

MAY 6th

JUNE 3rd

JULY 1st

AUGUST 5th

SEPTEMBER 2nd

Silhouette Desire

Now Available

Come Back, My Love by Pamela Wallace

TV newsperson Toni Lawrence was on the fast track to fame when photographer Theo Chakiris swept her off her feet at the Royal Wedding. Storybook romances belonged to princes and princesses! She tried to forget, to bury herself in her work, but passion brought them together to recapture the glory of ecstasy.

Blanket Of Stars by Lorraine Valley

Greece was the perfect setting for adventure and romance, and for Gena Fielding it became the land she would call home. In Alex Andreas' dark eyes she saw a passion and a glory, a flame to light the way to sensual pleasures and melt her resistance beneath the searing Greek sun.

Sweet Bondage by Dorothy Vernon

Maxwell Ross had set into motion a plan to avenge his younger brother. But he was wreaking revenge on the wrong woman, as Gemma Coleridge was only too happy to tell him—at first. But soon, too soon, her heart overrode her head. She lost her anger in Maxwell's arms, and dared to dream of a happiness that would last forever.

Silhouette Desire

Now Available

Dream Come True by Ann Major

Six years after their divorce, Barron Skymaster, superstar, tried to claim Amber again. But how could she face him after denying him knowledge of his own son—a son he had every right to know? Would that knowledge bring them together again or would it tear them apart forever?

Of Passion Born by Suzanne Simms

Professor Chelsie McBride was thoroughly acquainted with her subject—the sometimes humorous, sometimes bawdy Canterbury Tales. A respected professional in her field, she was no stranger to the earthy side of passion. But when it was introduced to her in the person of Drew Bradford, she realized she'd only been studying love by the book.

Second Harvest by Erin Ross

The fields of Kia Ora were all that remained of Alex's turbulent past, and Lindsay was bound to honour her husband's memory by taking an active part in the New Zealand vineyard. But what she began with reluctance soon became a fervent obsession. The exotic splendour of Kia Ora was captivating, and Philip Macek, its hard-driving owner, held her spellbound.

Silhouette Desire

Coming Next Month

Lover In Pursuit by Stephanie James

Reyna McKenzie vowed she'd never again succumb to Trevor Langdon's promise of love. But he'd come to Hawaii determined to reclaim her and under the tropical sun, she soon found herself willing to submit to the love she so desperately wanted.

King of Diamonds by Penny Allison

Carney Gallagher was baseball's golden boy, now in the troubled last season. Flame-haired Jo Ryan, the Atlanta *Star's* rookie woman sports reporter, made her first career hit at his expense. Gallagher vowed to even the score . . . but Jo never imagined that passion would be the weapon of his choice.

Love In The China Sea by Judith Baker

Kai Shanpei, mysterious Eurasian tycoon, was as much a part of Hong Kong as its crescent harbour, teeming streets and the jagged mountains looming above. From the moment she met him Anne Hunter was lost in his spell, plucked from reality and transported into his arms to learn the secrets of love.

Silhouette Desire

Coming Next Month

Bittersweet In Bern by Cheryl Durrant

Gabi Studer couldn't resist Peter Imhof's offer of work in Switzerland, but she hadn't reckoned on living in the same magnificent Alpine chalet as the famed author. Alone together on the enchanted Swiss mountainside, temptation was only a kiss away.

Constant Stranger by Linda Sunshine

Murphy Roarke literally knocked Joanna Davenport off her feet. She'd come to New York to launch a publishing career, and Roarke had helped her every step of the way . . . until he stole her heart, demanding that she choose between the job of a lifetime and a stormy, perilous love.

Shared Moments by Mary Lynn Baxter

He was the devil in disguise. Kace McCord, the silver-haired client Courtney Roberts tried to keep at arm's length. But he took possession of her from the first, arousing her feelings and driving her to heights of rapture.

Silhouette Desire

THE MORE SENSUAL PROVOCATIVE ROMANCE

95p each

1 ☐ **CORPORATE AFFAIR**
Stephanie James

2 ☐ **LOVE'S SILVER WEB**
Nicole Monet

3 ☐ **WISE FOLLY**
Rita Clay

4 ☐ **KISS AND TELL**
Suzanne Carey

5 ☐ **WHEN LAST WE LOVED**
Judith Baker

6 ☐ **A FRENCH-MAN'S KISS**
Kathryn Mallory

7 ☐ **NOT EVEN FOR LOVE**
Erin St. Claire

8 ☐ **MAKE NO PROMISES**
Sherry Dee

9 ☐ **MOMENT IN TIME**
Suzanne Simms

10 ☐ **WHENEVER I LOVE YOU**
Alana Smith

11 ☐ **VELVET TOUCH**
Stephanie James

12 ☐ **THE COWBOY AND THE LADY**
Diana Palmer

13 ☐ **COME BACK MY LOVE**
Pamela Wallace

14 ☐ **BLANKET OF STARS**
Lorraine Valley

15 ☐ **SWEET BONDAGE**
Dorothy Vernon

16 ☐ **DREAM COME TRUE**
Ann Major

17 ☐ **OF PASSION BORN**
Suzanne Simms

18 ☐ **SECOND HARVEST**
Erin Ross

All these books are available at your local bookshop or newsagent, or can be ordered direct from the publisher. Just tick the titles you want and fill in the form below.

Prices and availability subject to change without notice.

SILHOUETTE BOOKS, P.O. Box 11, Falmouth, Cornwall.

Please send cheque or postal order, and allow the following for postage and packing:

U.K. – 45p for one book, plus 20p for the second book, and 14p for each additional book ordered up to a £1.63 maximum.

B.F.P.O. and EIRE – 45p for the first book, plus 20p for the second book, and 14p per copy for the next 7 books, 8p per book thereafter.

OTHER OVERSEAS CUSTOMERS – 75p for the first book, plus 21p per copy for each additional book.

Name ....

Address ....

....